DON'T FALL IN LOVE

and how to break the rules

The Second Chance Chronicles

Book 2

SALLY BROOKS

ACKROYD
PUBLISHING

Ackroyd Publishing

ackroydpublishing.com

DON'T FALL IN LOVE

Prologue

SUMMER 2002

C hrissie and Nisha lay side by side on the lawn, wearing one ear bud each, listening to *Complicated* by Avril Lavigne on Nisha's Discman. It was after ten pm and dark, but the recent scorching weather meant it was still humid enough to be out in shorts and vest tops.

The Birmingham traffic was slowing, and the night was becoming quieter. Chrissie's long tanned thigh nestled comfortably against Nisha's more muscular one, her brown skin still glistening from the sun cream she'd applied earlier.

Chrissie loved these moments. A Levels were over at last. The night was opening out in front of them. They would lie there together, no need to speak. Chrissie felt a sense of quiet excitement deep in her stomach. It filled her up, and she smiled.

"What are you grinning about?" asked Nisha, not needing to look across to know.

"I'm just happy," said Chrissie. "Aren't you?"

"Well," said Nisha, pressing pause on the Discman and pushing herself up on one elbow, "I would be if we could find some ice-cream. Do you reckon we could raid your freezer?"

Chrissie laughed. "I'm in. Let's go."

From the kitchen, Chrissie looked out of the window into the garden where they had – literally – set up camp for the last few days. An old seventies ridge tent stood proud in the middle of the lawn, a dark triangle in the night. Her dad didn't seem to mind that she'd relocated, now that her exams were over. His only stipulation was that they should ensure they raise the ground sheet for a few hours each day to prevent the grass going yellow. He was proud of his garden.

Nisha rummaged in the freezer and pulled out a rectangular plastic container. "Oooh," she said, "Neapolitan ice-cream! My mum used to give me this when I was little. Old school."

"Oh God," said Chrissie, her long blonde hair hanging in waves down her back. "That's probably been in there since you were tiny – or at least shorter than you are now!"

Nisha poked Chrissie in the side before speaking. "Nah," she said, spoon already in her mouth. "It's good. Come on." She grinned, and Chrissie was struck again by the way her diminutive size somehow accentuated the force of her smile and personality. The strength she had gained from playing football showed, too.

"Tent?" enquired Chrissie.

"Tent," agreed Nisha.

They climbed into the orange tent, which still had a slightly musty smell. Chrissie's parents had used it frequently during the seventies and eighties, before she was born. Over the past few days she'd slowly moved cushions, books, blankets, a couple of torches and some battery-powered fairy-lights in. Her bedroom had become a place for revising for the dreaded A Level exams, or stressing about the same. Once the exams had finished, with the weather still swelter- ing, she had moved out of the house. Or at least ten metres or so out. It felt like freedom. She hadn't needed to actually invite Nisha to join her. It was an unspoken agreement.

The ice-cream had the slight taste of freezer burn, and was more than a little frosty, but in the tent, surrounded by twinkling lights, it didn't matter.

It was theirs.

"Ice-cream is so much better now it isn't accompanied by calculus and lack-of-revision remorse," said Nisha.

"Shudder. Agreed. Although I continue to be pleased I never studied maths. I mean, what were you thinking?" Chrissie poked Nisha, who giggled.

"It's a beautiful thing, when you don't have to do exams in it," she said, batting Chrissie's hand away, and then grab- bing it.

Chrissie's stomach flipped. The closeness between the two of them had been growing in the last few days, and last night there had been a moment when Nisha looked at her in a way that drew Chrissie in.

Chrissie knew she liked girls, had known for a while. But she hadn't really talked to anyone about it. School wasn't a forgiving place. But last night, every fibre in her body had screamed at her to kiss Nisha. The air between them had thinned, and Nisha's brown eyes had sparkled. Chrissie had taken a breath, and moved a millimetre towards Nisha, who suddenly looked away. The moment was lost. But then, in the night, Nisha's hand had found Chrissie's, and when Chrissie had woken this morning it had still been there. The two of them had slept the whole night side by side, hand in hand.

There was something apart from the real world about

these days in the tent. Nisha seemed more relaxed than she ever did at school, fiddling with her dark hair less and smiling more, the dimple on one side of her face showing.

This evening, Nisha still had Chrissie's hand. The grab turned into a gentler hold. And Chrissie squeezed, softly. No words had been spoken, but there seemed to be a revision essay's worth of words exchanged between the two girls.

Chrissie waited. She had never known Nisha to be inter- ested in anyone – boy or girl – and wasn't sure what this was. She looked shyly at Nisha, their eyes meeting. There was something different about Nisha this time, and the familiar thinning of the air and the instinct to move closer returned.

Then there was a deafening crash of thunder.

Chapter One

Glue sticks, round-ended scissors, pencils and exercise books were arranged in neat piles along child-sized desks. Chrissie surveyed the afternoon's work, finding a meditative calm in creating order out of chaos, safe in the knowledge that chaos would return in just thirty-six hours.

The final days before the start of the Autumn term were full of meetings, to-do lists and endless tasks. The classroom was pleasingly bare, probably for the last time before next summer. Chrissie breathed out, allowing her eyelids to close over hazel eyes, flexing her neck as she sat on a child's chair with her knees almost meeting her ears. She reflected, as she did most days, that this was not a healthy position to work in.

When she opened her eyes Mrs Hemingway was standing in the doorway. "Indeed, Miss Anderson. I often feel the same way at this time of day." Chrissie snapped to attention, no mean feat in her tiny chair.

"Sorry, I was just taking a moment," said Chrissie.

"I'd say taking moments like that when you can is a wise

move." Mrs Hemingway walked towards Chrissie, pulled up a tiny chair and sat beside her. Somehow she managed to remain dignified – or at least more dignified than Chrissie. "As you know," she said, "this will be Year Four's classroom this year, and you have a new teacher. It's all been a little last-minute after Mr Sykes' unexpected retirement." She grimaced at Chrissie, who wasn't sure how she should react. "Because we had to leave it so late to recruit our new teacher, he wasn't able to be here today, as you can see."

Chrissie nodded. She could see.

Mrs Hemingway continued: "But he will be here tomorrow, thank goodness. It does mean you'll both have to work swiftly on any displays for the children in time for the first day of term, though."

Chrissie had already thought this through, hence her work to get everything else as close to ready as possible for the new classroom. She was keen to get away to her yoga class and re-centre herself in preparation for tomorrow's new arrival. She hoped that whoever he was, he'd be good to work with. She'd adored working with Dan Harvey last term and was sad that the inevitable annual reshuffle meant she would be with someone new.

"Mr Rangan comes highly recommended from a London school, and has excellent experience. I'm sure you will be able to welcome him and get him settled in quickly," said the head teacher.

"It will all be fine," replied Chrissie. "It sounds like he won't need too much help from me." She looked around the room, beginning to think through how she would apply her creative abilities to the classroom displays.

"Jolly good," said Mrs Hemingway, her voice warm, the blue plastic beads from circa 1987 clacking around her neck. She was the kind of woman who seemed ageless. She could be anything from mid-forties to mid-sixties. "You've become such an asset to the school, Miss Anderson. It's only been a year, but already I can see other teaching assistants looking to you for guidance." She smoothed her skirt, stood up, gave Chrissie a firm nod, and left the room.

Chrissie wondered what Mr Rangan would be like. There was a knot of apprehension in her stomach. He had been recruited at relatively short notice. What was the likelihood that he would actually be outstanding – either by Ofsted's standards, or Chrissie's? Teachers with stunning resumés and terrible skills were a well-known phenomenon – how else would a school ensure the swift departure of a team member they wanted to say goodbye to? She sighed to herself. Pondering on it wouldn't help.

Once she was confident that all the equipment was ready, Chrissie looked up at the clock. It was past four. Time to get going. She gathered her possessions and pulled a light cotton scarf around her neck. She left the school and was soon on Kings Heath High Street. It was buzzing with adults taking children to buy new shoes, stationery and clothing. There was a long queue outside the school uniform shop, a line of stressed parents and bored-looking children. A few children waved at Chrissie, shouting out "Hi, Miss, see you at school!" She smiled warmly and waved, but she knew better than to stop and talk. There would be plenty of time for that at school, and this was her time now.

As she approached the village square, two number 50 buses parked up at the bus stop nearby, she felt herself begin to relax. This was where she could come to release the worries of the mundane world.

The community centre beside the church in the heart of Kings Heath was slightly shabby, but it was home to Chrissie's yoga class. The range of abilities in the class was wide, but it was a warm, welcoming space, and the teacher made everyone feel at home. Rae had a way of making them all feel like yoga was for them, while bringing a sense of calm to their class.

Chrissie breathed into downward dog. This was the last vestige of her old life, the only part she hadn't discarded for her own wellbeing – and that of those around her. Rae's down-to-earth nature had made yoga a safe place for her again. There were no smells and chimes and none of the ideological chatter that had taken her to a dark place before, and for that she was grateful. She had learned the hard way that there was no simple answer to life, no matter how confidently someone tried to explain it.

The cat, cow, cat routine eased her hips after all the crouching and organising cupboards during the day. The warrior poses helped her feel strong, prepared, capable.

"And now," said Rae, "I want you all to gently lie down on your mats, breathing deeply, and take that shavasana that you have worked for over the last forty-five minutes or so." Chrissie could hear the sounds of people exhaling, relaxing, letting go. Shavasana, or corpse pose, was always the highlight of any class. It meant lying still on your back with your eyes shut. Chrissie had often wondered at the fact that you could lie down anywhere, at any time, but it would never feel as good as the moment when you'd finished a yoga class and were lying still like this.

Chrissie exhaled, her eyes closed, enjoying the sensation of her body stopping after the exertions of the class. Newcomers were often shocked by how strenuous yoga could be. Her face felt warm, and there was a sheen of perspiration on it. Her legs welcomed the break, and she sensed she was regaining some energy and spark after her long day at work.

"And slowly, in your own time," said Rae, their voice barely above a whisper in the silent room, "I want you to come to a sitting position. Yes, that's right. Bring your palms together and in front of your face and be grateful to yourself for giving your body this session to strengthen and grow. Namaste."

"Namaste," said Chrissie under her breath.

Once the class was done, mat rolled up and socks and shoes back on, and feeling lighter and more centred than she had earlier, she smiled and offered to help Rae tidy up.

"Thanks, Chrissie," said Rae, their short curly hair slightly damp from the exertion of the class. Somehow they'd managed to demonstrate and talk the class through all the movements, and end up significantly less sweaty than Chrissie was, though. "Cup of tea?"

They parked themselves on the side in the suitably municipal kitchen, complete with labels for each cupboard shelf. Sipping from light green institutional teacups, the two of them exchanged stories about their respective days.

"It sounds like you've found your feet at the school," said Rae, nodding their head in the direction of Chrissie's workplace.

"Yes," Chrissie agreed, smiling and remembering Mrs Hemingway's words. "I really think I might have."

"You should be so proud of all you've achieved," said Rae, nudging Chrissie's elbow. "Think about where you were. I remember how pale and quiet you were when you first came to my class. Now look at you." They smiled broadly. "Positively blooming."

"Thanks, Rae. Well, I do really have you to thank," said Chrissie, her voice quiet, mindful that while Rae knew some of the story, they didn't know everything, or how quite bad things had got in the last few years. They didn't know how much Chrissie had lost, and how much she had to atone for. "You met me where I was and helped me make sense of a few things. I wasn't sure I'd be able to come back to yoga, but here we are. Thank you."

"You did it," said Rae, "I just get the pleasure of witnessing you." They smiled.

Chapter Two

It was the day before the start of term and the sun was shining, echoes of summer still in the air. Chrissie sat at the small desk in her living room, looking out at the tree that stood between her window and the road. In front of her was an A4 hardbound journal, black and well-thumbed, with many pages already full.

Chrissie opened it and started to set out her intentions for the day, always keeping her three rules at the forefront of her mind – the rules she had set down for herself to ensure she didn't fall back into the chaos her life had become. She had come up with them as guiding principles to keep order and sanity in her life. But more than that, they were there to stop her from hurting anyone ever again:

One – Don't fall in love.

Two – Question everything.

Three – Give back.

Today's focus was on being ready and willing to welcome Mr Rangan into the school, whatever he might be like. She needed to remember to listen, to understand and to give something of herself to benefit others. She wrote everything down, and then underlined a few words with a green glittery gel pen. When she had chosen the book, she had deliberately opted for plain black, to avoid distraction and provide herself with a blank slate, quite literally. But she couldn't resist the glittery gel pens. They made her smile. And she didn't think they could do her any harm.

She wrote about the past day or so, about all that had happened at school, in yoga. She reflected on her conversation with Rae. She couldn't help but think back to her younger self. September always seemed to be a time of comparisons – her first day at secondary school, her first day at university, her first day at her workplace a year earlier. A time of new starts. She pictured herself at eighteen, preparing to leave home, readying herself for university with her dad by her side, nursing a broken heart that she didn't think she could tell him about.

She sighed. Her dad. What would he have thought of the last few years? She felt a lump in her throat, but swallowed it, returning to her journal.

She had started again. She had made things good. Yes, she still needed to do more, but things were so much better now than they had been.

Absentmindedly, Chrissie drew a spiral that took up the corner of the page. She wouldn't allow her life to spiral again, she knew that for sure. She closed the book, placed her hand on the cover for a moment, and then put it into her bag.

It was an early start, but the brightness of the morning made it worthwhile. There weren't many people about at half past seven when she left her flat, and she luxuriated in the relative peace. The high street was only a few minutes' walk away, and there were inevitable delivery vans, buses and cars, but for bustling Kings Heath, this was quiet.

Chrissie got to her classroom before the new teacher, which was her aim. She wanted to get herself organised and ready for the day. She knew she needed to be welcoming to him and make sure everything went well, ready for the children arriving the following day. She smiled to herself and went to the staff room to make a cup of peppermint tea. There were a few staff already there, photocopying, looking at their laptops, making notes. She smiled and helloed her way in and out, keen to get started on the day's tasks.

She walked back through the doors of her classroom to find that the new teacher must have arrived in her absence – there was a jacket slung over the back of one of the chairs. Mr Rangan was obviously an early bird too, which boded well.

Chrissie could see a figure bent over and peering into one of the cupboards she'd tidied the day before.

"Hi," said Chrissie, putting on her best welcoming grin.

The figure straightened. He was shorter than Chrissie had expected, his hair shoulder-length and dark. As he turned, Chrissie realised he wasn't a 'he' at all.

"Hi," said the woman standing in front of her, her mouth dropping open.

If the person in front of her faltered, then something inside Chrissie screamed to a shuddering halt. Visions of a seventies ridge tent in the middle of a lawn sprang unbidden into her mind. Ice-cream. A battered old Discman. She felt herself reel a little and step back, as though she had been physically pushed into the past.

"Nisha?" asked Chrissie, although she already knew the answer. It was pulsing through her veins.

"Chrissie!" said Nisha, smiling broadly, her eyes wide. "I had no idea you worked here."

She still had the dimple.

"Well, I do," said Chrissie, immediately wishing she had said something more interesting. She felt like she was watching the scenario play out, rather than being part of it. She rested her hand on a bookshelf, in search of stability, accidentally knocking down a copy of *The Day the Crayons Quit*. "I mean, I've worked here for about a year."

"You're a teacher too?" asked Nisha, one hand playing with the strap of her smart watch, her wavy hair falling into her face.

"Ah, no," said Chrissie, bending to retrieve the book and trying to take a moment to centre herself while she was near the ground. She stood up slowly, hoping not to knock anything else over. "I'm a teaching assistant." She took a breath.

"Well, what a turnout," said Nisha, who was looking around the room, as if trying to find an explanation for this unexpected turn of events. Chrissie wondered which class Nisha would be teaching, and where Mr Rangan might be. This was truly awkward, and she was desperate for the moment to end.

"Yes," said Chrissie. "It's a surprise. So, what year group are you teaching this year? Or are you doing supply or something?"

"No, I'm permanent," said Nisha. "I'm teaching Year Four."

"Oh, I think there's been a mistake," said Chrissie, still hoping Mr Rangan would appear at any point. "Mr Rangan is the teacher for Year Four this year. He's new. Not here yet." She looked over her shoulder, willing the elusive Mr Rangan to appear.

Nisha pressed her lips together. "Ah. Yes. Well," she said, slowly, "you're right, there has been a mistake. Everything was done in a rush. I am, as I'm sure you'll remember, Nisha Rajan – Ms Rajan. Somewhere along the lines a mistake was made in the documentation. One Asian surname apparently looks and sounds very much like another." Nisha rolled her eyes. "And in the same mix-up, I also became a 'Mr' by mistake."

Dread gathered in Chrissie's stomach. "Oh. Yes, I see. How annoying for you."

Nisha sighed. "To be honest, I'm just grateful I was able to get a job at such relative short notice. Anyway, which class do you work with?"

Chrissie girded her loins. "Er, Year Four. Your class." Chrissie felt the words echo around the room. Every day for the best part of the next year, they would be working together. She was suddenly aware of her heart beating faster than was healthy.

Nisha's eyes widened, and Chrissie couldn't help being reminded of the lingering looks they'd shared more than twenty years earlier. "Awesome," said Nisha, scraping her hair behind her ears and tying it back with a hairband she'd retrieved from her wrist. It was a trademark move, and one that Chrissie remembered well. It was as though nothing had changed.

But everything had changed.

"I only accepted the job here last week, and I didn't think I'd know anyone." She smiled, her dimple threading in and out of her cheek.

"Awesome," echoed Chrissie, although the word felt cumbersome in her mouth, like a dry cracker. "I, er, ought to go and get the photocopying I set up earlier. Back in a tick." She swiftly exited the room, forgetting her tea, and headed straight to the loos in the corridor. She found a cubicle, popped the toilet lid down and took a seat, and immediately regretted the decision to have a personal crisis on a child's toilet. Her knees were by her shoulders. She sighed and started the routine.

Rule one – don't fall in love. She thought of that night, the day's heat still rising from the earth, the smell of musty canvas, the tinny sound of Avil Lavigne from discarded earphones, and the sense that life would never be the same again. Then of the following morning. No, she was good. She wasn't in love. That was long ago.

Rule two – question everything. Nisha was back. Why? Why now? Could Chrissie work alongside her every day for the whole school year? What would that be like? Could they be friends after all this time? Should they be?

Rule three – give back. She had a duty to give Nisha a chance. Yes. A responsibility. She nodded to herself. This was the right thing to do. She imagined herself holding the hand of her eighteen-year-old self, reassuring her it wouldn't always hurt, and that one day she'd be able to meet Nisha and smile.

She grimaced.

Chapter Three

Rae and Chrissie were at a small vegetarian café on Kings Heath High Street, sharing some pitta bread and a vat of hummus.

"All set for the first day of term tomorrow, then?" asked Rae. They were still in their yoga clothes, their mats resting against the table.

Chrissie puffed out a breath. "Well, the glue sticks are all present and correct, the scissors and pencils and display boards are all up and ready. But I don't think I'd call myself ready, to be honest. I only met my new teacher today, and I'm not sure how it's going to work," she said, opting not to get into the detail of her situation.

"Oh, really," probed Rae. "How come?" They took a glug of water and trained their eyes on Chrissie, quizzically. "You've only just met them, and already you're not sure? That's not like you."

"Yeah, you're right, of course you're right. I ought not make any assumptions. I need to keep an open mind," said Chrissie. "She's just, um, different to what I'm used to."

"Ah," said Rae. "Well, different can be good. Sometimes it's something to learn from, right?"

"You are, as always, correct," said Chrissie, again impressed by the wisdom of her younger friend.

"Do you think it might be first day of term nerves?"

"It might," agreed Chrissie, knowing that it really wasn't, choosing not to expand any further. "It's going to be an interesting class. I helped out with them a bit last term when they were in Year Three and they were, well, let's just say they were a lively bunch."

"Ha," said Rae, "now there's a word doing some heavy lifting. 'Lively'. I'm sure you'll be equal to the task. You've taken on far bigger challenges." They gave Chrissie a firm stare and suddenly looked a lot more serious.

"Yes, I have," said Chrissie. Starting again had been hard, after all that had happened. She thought back to this time last year, finding somewhere to live, the counselling sessions, Kiera. Starting over is hard when your life has been burned down. Especially when you're the one who lit the match.

"You have," confirmed Rae, bringing Chrissie back from her wandering thoughts. Chrissie gave a weak smile.

On the way home to her flat, on the ground floor of a large Edwardian terrace, she reviewed her day. Following their initial meeting, Nisha had seemed busy until they left after five pm. She was in and out of meetings, staring at her laptop screen through large reading glasses, wearing a serious expression throughout. As they'd both left for the day, Nisha had turned to her and said, "We should catch up properly, over a drink sometime." She smiled that smile again, broad and open, that dimple returning again from all those years ago. But was there something a little more guarded in her old friend than Chrissie remembered?

"We should," responded Chrissie, her neck prickling. She wasn't sure where on earth they would start when it came to 'catching up'. Two decades was a long time to catch up on, especially after the way things had been left. Escaping to Rae's yoga class had been a blessing.

When she got home, Chrissie found herself streaming Escapology by Robbie Williams, one of the albums that had been on permanent replay that summer. The song *Feel* took on a new meaning now, with its plea to find real love.

But Chrissie knew love wasn't for her. Rule one: Don't fall in love. Not after everything that had happened. Not after everything she had done.

Still, she couldn't bring herself to skip the track.

She returned to her journal and worked through the events of the day, writing everything down methodically with a turquoise gel pen. Turquoise was calming, right? The colour of the cosmos, or so she'd read online.

Chrissie allowed her mind to wander back to that summer, to the conversations late into the night, the smell of the dying embers of neighbours' barbecues, the feel of the synthetic sleeping bags. She wondered if it was just her who remembered everything in such minute detail. She'd felt like life had changed forever that summer. A levels seemed irrelevant, and she dedicated more of her time to Nisha than she did to the French texts she should have been studying. She smiled to herself. She'd scraped the grades she needed for university, and that night she and Nisha had decided to celebrate.

And then, things changed.

Chrissie looked down. She found she'd absentmindedly been doodling Nisha's name over and over again – *Nisha Rajan*, *Nisha Rajan*, *Nisha Rajan*. She had swirled lines around the letters, turning it into a mandala. She froze and gripped her pen tightly.

She reminded herself. Rule two: Question everything. Why was Nisha back? Why was she going to be working so closely with Chrissie? Could it really just be chance? Did Nisha know how far into Chrissie's throat her heart had leapt? Did Nisha remember the past the same way Chrissie did? Had she felt the same shock at meeting again?

She listed these questions, one by one, with a purple asterisk next to each. Most of them had no answers, but putting them on the page helped.

Then, as routine dictated, time for rule three: Give back.

Tomorrow was the first day of term. The children would be returning from their summer breaks. Many would be tanned and happy from family time away in the sunshine. Some would have spent the few weeks helping care for members of their family, or perhaps finding a safe place amid chaos and difficulty. The summer holidays were a mixed blessing. Children and staff looked forward to them so much, but on return, some children would be in desperate need of routine, support, reliable grown-ups, and in some cases, food.

Chrissie took out her phone and texted Dan Harvey. He'd been looking for volunteers for breakfast club. This was part of a drive to ensure every child had something in their stomach to start the day. She confirmed she'd be there at half past seven, ready and willing with a plastic apron and catering gloves.

She went to bed trying not to think about the year ahead, and the time she would be spending with Nisha.

Chapter Four

The sun was shining again, which always made the first day of term a little easier. Chrissie had decided today was a new day. She and Nisha were adults now, in their forties. They had lived multitudes of lives since their teens and could absolutely work together effectively and professionally. She arrived in the school kitchen at half past seven, as promised, to find Dan already laying out loaves of bread and vast quantities of margarine.

"Morning, sunshine," he said, smiling as he spoke. "Glad I'm not the only girly swot in today."

"You can count on me, Dan. Love the jumper, by the way," said Chrissie, admiring the pink and yellow V-neck he sported.

"Thanks. I always like to welcome the newbies with a bit of colour." He pulled the lid off one of the massive cartons of marg with gusto, then dropped eight slices of toast into the two large toasters that had been donated.

"You've got Reception this year, then?" asked Chrissie, as she started getting the plates ready.

"Yep, God love 'em." Dan twinkled as he spoke. He was one of those teachers who seemed to genuinely love the job. It could be a thankless profession at times, but he never seemed to let the stress get to him. He was often the first in in the morning, and it had been Dan that had done the deal with local supermarkets to provide breakfast supplies every day. This was their second year doing breakfast club.

"Whereas I've got Year Four this time."

"Hmmm," said Dan, pulling open another loaf of bread. "All the gear and no idea? Yes, I remember that agegroup. Always entertaining. They're beginning to feel like they're all grown up…"

"And yet," said Chrissie, buttering like fury.

"… they are utterly clueless," concluded Dan. "But still, you're less likely to be clearing up puddles on the classroom floor than I am." He paused to reload the toasters, while Chrissie popped the buttered toast under the hot lamps. "So, I gather we have fresh meat teaching Year Four this year."

"Oh my God, Dan. Fresh meat?"

Dan giggled. "OK, I'm just trying to make things more interesting. So, what's she like? I saw her briefly in a meeting yesterday, but she didn't say much. She's going to be your work-wife this year, so you must have views."

Chrissie felt the heat spread across her face, and looked down to focus on her margarine-spreading.

"For what it's worth," added Dan, "she looks like just your type."

"Oh my God, Dan, again, we are in a place where children are being educated and enriched, calm down!" Chrissie pursed her lips, aware that he was right. "To be fair," she continued, "I've not had a chance to talk to her much. She was very busy yesterday. She's not really a super-chatty person."

"Ah, so you've gleaned that much already," said Dan, putting a pile of freshly toasted bread at Chrissie's side.

She sighed, deciding that less was more. "Well, that's how she seemed to me."

"Here we are," came a voice from the other side of the hatch that opened into the school hall. "I'm sure Miss Anderson and her friend will be able to find you some yummy toast, and that's bound to help, isn't it?" Chrissie looked up to see Nisha, shepherding towards them a small boy with the red eyes of someone who'd just been crying.

Chrissie caught her breath, hoping Nisha hadn't heard them gossiping about her, and noting her navy chinos and Converse. She smiled at Nisha and the boy. "This is Francis," said Nisha. "He's in our class, Miss Anderson."

Chrissie went mildly pink again. It was the first time she'd hear Nisha call her Miss Anderson, and it made her feel odd. She decided she didn't want to unpack that here and now.

"Hello, Francis," she said. "You must be new to the school. It's lovely to have you here."

The boy, who had refused to take off his coat, attempted to smile, but a tear fell down his cheek instead. Chrissie turned to Dan. "Mr Harvey, we have an urgent case of first day sadness. I think we need to deploy the emergency chocolate spread!"

Nisha threw Chrissie a grateful smile, and for a moment a small grin appeared on Francis' face. "Chocolate spread is my favourite," he said, his voice only just above a whisper.

The boy was quickly furnished with two pieces of toast heavily endowed with both margarine and '*Notella*' – an imitation of the original which cost a fraction of the real thing. His eyes grew large when he saw them, and Nisha put a reassuring hand on his shoulder as he began to tuck in.

Once Francis was settled, Nisha walked over to the hatch. "Thanks," she said. She smiled at Chrissie and then proffered her hand across the counter towards Dan. "I'm Nisha, by the way. Sorry I didn't get to properly introduce myself yesterday, it was all a bit hectic, but I'm pleased to meet you now, and thanks for the chocolate spread. I'm willing to take the inevitable sugar crash he'll have later if we can just stop him crying for a bit, poor thing."

Dan leaned over and shook her hand, grinning at her. "My pleasure. Great to have you aboard."

Francis began to relax, saying a few words here and there with Nisha's encouragement. Chrissie watched, impressed with her ability to nurture the frightened child. The boy was encouraged to finish off his toast quickly, before the other children arrived and all wanted chocolate toast. Dan had limited resources, so the spread was kept on the down-low, for extreme cases only.

Before long they were inundated with children scoffing their toast with gusto. Time was ticking, and there was lots to be done, so Chrissie began to clear up. She knew she had to be in the Year Four classroom shortly.

"So, how many small countries do you think we could feed with the leftover crusts?" asked Nisha, who had stayed to help, having introduced Francis to some other children.

"I'm thinking Luxemburg," said Chrissie, giggling. Hungry or not, crusts remained a sticking point for many children.

"You're good with the kids," Nisha observed, smiling at Chrissie. "I never thought of you doing this sort of thing. Have you been doing it long?"

Chrissie paused, a pile of plates in her hands. "No, only a year or so. It was a bit of a change of direction, really."

"Interesting," said Nisha. "You can tell me more about that later." She raised an eyebrow and turned to sweep more crusts into the rubbish bag Chrissie was holding. Chrissie frowned. She wasn't sure she wanted to tell Nisha any more than that.

Chrissie joined Dan as they tidied up the kitchen. "She seems alright," said Dan, nodding his head towards Nisha. "You can never tell with last minute hires. One always needs to ask – why were they available at such short notice?"

"Er, yeah, I guess. She's fine, I think," said Chrissie, who was still trying to work out how she felt about Nisha's sudden reinsertion into her life.

"You ok?" asked Dan, picking up on Chrissie's ambivalence.

"Yeah, sorry, first day, lots to think about," she replied.

"Take it easy."

Chapter Five

"Good morning, class 4R," said Nisha. "Let's get ourselves sat down nicely in our places." Chrissie was handing out name stickers and helping the children find their seats. "Dottie, I can see toast crumbs all down your front, can you brush yourself down, please?"

Dottie was a name she was confident Nisha would be saying a lot in class, and possibly with a hint of frustration in her voice. Chrissie smiled. Dottie was a bright spark in the class, in all ways, and prone to a bit of chatter and chaos.

"Thank you," said Nisha, as the noise settled. "I want to introduce myself to you, because you all know each other and the school – in most cases," she looked warmly over at Francis, who still looked a little terrified. "My name is Ms Rajan and I'm brand new," she said, "so I will be learning from you." She paused. "But," she paused again, this time for emphasis, and adopted a very serious expression, "we are class 4R, and we are awesome."

Chrissie could hear children giggling. Nisha continued. "So," another dramatic pause, silencing the children, "in the mornings, when you come in, I want you to remember that. Can you remember that?"

There was a low murmur across the room.

Nisha raised her voice. "I can't hear you. Can you remember that?"

"Yes," said a few voices.

"Hmmm," said Nisha, "Miss Anderson, I think we can do better than that, don't you?"

Chrissie nodded, "Oh yes, Miss, I think so."

"Good," said Nisha, looking at the wide-eyed children before her. "Repeat after me: We are class 4R, and we are awesome!" The children hesitated. "Come on!"

"We are class 4R and we are awesome," said the children quietly.

"You don't sound awesome," observed Nisha, frowning. "Try again, and this time try and put a bit of oomph into it. I want Mr Harvey to have to pop his head in to find out why we're all being so noisy and awesome."

The children giggled, and this time they bellowed the words, looking at each other with smiles on their faces.

"Much better, thank you," said Nisha, turning her gaze to Chrissie. "Miss Anderson, I wonder if you could help us get started on our literacy this morning."

Nisha had a commanding presence in the classroom, and the children seemed to respond to it in spite of the inevitable first day excitement.

The morning passed in a whirl of handing out books and pencils, answering questions about whether or not Hardev's father really was Spiderman, as he insisted, and checking that Francis was getting on ok.

Lunchtime came as a welcome relief. "Well," said Nisha, "we made it. Well done, us."

"Half a day down, umpteen more to go," replied

Chrissie, with a laugh. Saying it out loud reminded her of the reality of her situation. "But yes, I think we got through ok. The children always struggle the first day back, particularly when it comes to sitting still and paying attention, so I reckon we did well. Aside from Dottie's lap of honour for getting all her maths questions right, at least."

Nisha laughed. "Coffee, I think."

They settled down together in the staff room. Chrissie was beginning to feel more comfortable with Nisha, although each time she thought back to that summer, a shudder tore through her heart. That couldn't go on all year, surely?

"Good afternoon, ladies," said Dan, settling himself down beside the two women with his Lego themed lunchbox.

"Hey, bab," said Chrissie, happy to have safer company.

"So, how was your morning?" asked Dan. Nisha took the opportunity to describe the Spiderman incident in all its glory, and the classroom drama that had followed. Chrissie allowed the conversation to flow over her as she ate the falafel salad she'd made that morning.

Her mind drifted to the many lunches of instant noodles she had shared with Nisha that July, once their A levels were over. They would sit on the lawn on a blanket, surrounded by books, talking endlessly about everything and nothing. It was a hot summer and it felt like it would never end. There was football on TV every day, constant stories about David Beckham and England's chances in the World Cup, Shakira and Coldplay on the radio, and they didn't have a care in the world. Until they did.

"So I realised then that I needed to make a change," said Nisha, her voice breaking into Chrissie's reverie.

"Yeah, I get that," said Dan, opening a tiny Tupperware box filled with grapes, and popping them into his mouth one by one.

"And this job came up. It seemed like a sign," Nisha went on. "After everything that happened, coming home didn't seem like such a bad thing to do. I was always happy in Birmingham."

"And who can resist the pull of the People's Republic of Kings Heath?" said Dan, smiling.

"Well, absolutely. Chrissie and I spent many happy days here when we were young."

Dan's head snapped up from his grapes. "You know each other?" he said. Chrissie froze.

"Yeah, we were at school together," Nisha replied casually.

Chrissie could hear the blood roaring in her ears. "A long time ago," she said.

Nisha frowned slightly and looked down at her own lunch. Dan eyed Chrissie quizzically before Nisha stood up. "I guess I should get set up for the afternoon," she said, almost sprinting for the exit.

"Now there is totally a story here," said Dan. "How is it that you omitted to tell me that you actually know her, that you were at school with her?"

Chrissie felt guilty. She should have been more open with her friend. "It's complicated," she replied.

"I'm not going to pry," said Dan, "much as I'd love to." He winked. "It's your business. But are you ok? You seem a bit off."

"I'm fine," Chrissie told him. "It was all a long time ago. We were friends and then had a bit of a bust up before we went to uni. We never saw each other again after that, so it's just a bit awkward to be honest." It wasn't the whole truth, but it wasn't a lie. "I'm sorry, Dan. I should have told you I knew her."

"Don't worry, bab," he said, "we all have our secrets."

Chrissie was relieved. Dan was a good friend. She didn't want to lose him.

Chapter Six

"Do you ever think about what happened to the others?" asked Rae.

Chrissie and Rae were having a glass of wine together in the Vine on Kings Heath High Street. It was midweek, and just beginning to get dark outside. There was always a mixed crowd in the café bar, representing the diversity of the south Birmingham neighbourhood that boasted its own, albeit tiny, Pride parade.

"Yes," said Chrissie, more open than usual, thanks to the two glasses of sauvignon blanc she'd already imbibed. "I think about Athena."

"Your ex?" said Rae.

"Yeah. I wonder what happened to her. She left before I did, but I've not seen her since. I'm glad she got out. I do worry about the others, though."

Chrissie couldn't help thinking about Athena from time to time. Athena was the woman she'd developed a relationship with, just as her marriage was falling apart. It had been ill-advised, but it was a symptom of the destructive way in which she was living her life at the time.

"I guess the thing with cults is that people often join them of their own free will, or at least, that's how it feels to them," Rae observed.

Chrissie winced at the word 'cult'. It had taken her months to acknowledge that she had been part of one, or even say the word out loud. It had been just over a year since she'd extricated herself from Infinite Bliss. And if she was honest, it had been more an escape than an extrication, because she had been in danger. She pursed her lips before speaking. "Yes. That's it. I thought I was being empowered, but in fact I was taking my power and giving it to someone else."

"Lucian," said Rae, recalling the name of the charismatic leader.

"Yeah. He made everything seem so easy," said Chrissie, looking out of the window. "To start with, at least. He had an explanation for everything. It started with what he called 'hyper-connected body movement' which, looking back, was a travesty of true yoga." She remembered the classes, the chimes, the chanting, the incense, the answers. The most pervasive thing was the answers. Lucian could explain suffering, pain, happiness and give a path to a better life. He was offering certainty, community, and joy, and it was an irresistible combination.

And, inevitably, it was too good to be true. But at the time, it had tempted Chrissie away from the mundanity of her life.

"In believing in him, I destroyed my own life." Chrissie paused for a moment. "And someone else's." She saw the question in Rae's eyes, and moved on quickly. "So now I have a duty to be better, to give more, to consider others, to question things."

Rae frowned for a moment, as though trying to make up their mind about something. "Well," they said, "I think we can all do more of that." They put out their hand and rested it on Chrissie's. "I've not known you long, but I can tell you that you're a very good friend, that you're generous and caring, in spite of your obsession with glitter gel pens." Rae winked and Chrissie laughed.

"I love those pens – and my journal. It all keeps me on the straight and narrow." She dropped her hand to the messenger bag beside her, where her journal sat, with her at all times. "And who doesn't love the chance to buy stationery?"

"You are living your best life, queen," said Rae, their eyes glittering. They ran their hands through their brown curls. "Ugh, I need a haircut."

"But don't cut off the mullet, bab," said Chrissie, a teasing note in her voice.

"Never," agreed Rae, laughing.

"I love that mullets are back in fashion. I remember the early noughties when David Beckham kicked off the resurgence. Things do have a tendency to come back round."

"Tell me more, Grandma." Rae was only in their mid-twenties, and had no recollection of those heady days. Or maybe they were only heady to Chrissie because she had been in her late teens. Because of that summer. And Nisha.

Chrissie laughed. "Ah well, young one, those were the days of Big Brother, Pop Idol, Shakira, Michael Owen, Avril Lavigne…" She tried a soulful gaze, into the middle distance, but couldn't keep the grin from her lips.

"Yeah, those are just words, Chrissie," said Rae.

"Well, my sweet summer child, it gets curiouser still. Let

me tell you about the era when all your mobile phone could do was make calls and text messages – text messages you paid for each time you sent one. It was a simpler time…"

"Ok, Granny, much as I'd love to sit and hear more of your fireside tales of the golden olden days, I do need to get going. I've got an early start tomorrow," said Rae, draining their glass and putting their jacket on. The September air had a chill in it.

"You go. I plan to rest my not-so-young bones for a little longer while I finish my drink and contemplate whether I, too, need a mullet," said Chrissie.

"Nope," replied Rae. "You're not allowed. This is all too lovely." They gestured towards Chrissie's long, flowing, dirty blonde waves. Chrissie smiled.

"Why, thank you. I'll see you shortly, I'm sure. Just as soon as I've collected my pension." Rae laughed, gave Chrissie a quick hug, and then left.

Chrissie looked into her wine glass, and unbidden, her mind flew back to those days after the exams were over. She and Nisha would lie out on the blanket Chrissie had pinched from her dad's car boot. It was one of those old-style red-and-black tartan woollen ones, that had been used in her family since the seventies. It smelled of the car and the beach and her childhood.

They would each have a book to read and a glass of some kind of fizzy pop. Every now and again one of them would shift position, or exclaim out loud at a passage in their book. Chrissie smiled to herself. She was a frequent visitor – and contributor – to BookTok, and it struck her that the way the two of them read side by side, sharing their thoughts, was a very early – and very slow – version of the same thing.

She recalled one particular evening. The sun was going

down. "I've finished it," said Nisha. Chrissie looked across to her and spotted tears in her friend's eyes.

"Wow," said Chrissie, "nothing makes you cry. Like, ever!"

"Oh, it is so good! And so sad," said Nisha, smiling and crying at the same time. She closed the book and handed it to Chrissie. *The Lovely Bones*, by Alice Sebold.

"Isn't that the one that starts with the murder of a young girl?" asked Chrissie, furrowing her brow. "I mean, call me a critic, but that doesn't sound very feminist."

"Oh, Chrissie, my friend, you absolutely have to read it. It's gorgeous and sad and wonderful and heartbreaking, and I may never get over it."

It wasn't like Nisha to gush like this. Chrissie tentatively took the book, but then laid it down beside her. "I'm still on this one," she said, holding up her latest charity shop find. It had dog-eared corners and a very worn spine.

"What is it?"

"*The Winds of Lake Calloway*. It's by R S Montague, whoever that is. Never heard of them," said Chrissie, who was only a few pages into a book that would start a chain of events that would alter the course of their summer, and perhaps her life.

Chapter Seven

"Bonjour, la classe," said Nisha to the children in front of her, who responded with a giggle.

She frowned.

"Ai-je dit quelque chose de drole?"

The class fell silent. Chrissie was standing at the back, attempting to hide a smile. This was Year Four's first French lesson, and Nisha had arrived that morning wearing a Breton striped blue and white top and a beret. She winked at the children and gave them a winning smile, then nodded at Chrissie, who had been briefed for today's antics.

"Good morning, class," Chrissie said, and the pupils whipped their heads around to face her. "I will interpret for Ms Rajan. She said hello to you all, and when you giggled, she asked if she had said something funny."

"Oui," said Nisha, smiling, allowing her dimple to show. Her black hair was shiny and set off the beret perfectly. She suited stripes, thought Chrissie, and immediately found herself wondering why she was paying so much attention to the way the teacher looked.

Chrissie walked to the front of the classroom and spoke. "Ms Rajan is speaking a different language this morning. Can any of you tell me what language she is speaking?" Dottie's hand went up straight away. Chrissie studiously avoided looking at her, as she was always the first with something to say. She looked over at Francis, who for the first time since he had arrived in the class had put his hand up. Or at least, he had lifted it very slightly off the table in front of him. He looked terrified, but she decided to take the risk and call on him to respond.

Francis spoke in no more than a whisper. "It's French, Miss." His face went bright red as all the children focused on him.

"Yes," said Chrissie, injecting as much positivity as she could into that one word. "Very good, Francis, that's exactly right." She looked across at Nisha, who smiled at her in silent celebration. It had been a week since Francis had joined the school, and he'd barely spoken a word. "I think that deserves a marble in the jar."

Nisha immediately went over to the shelf where the marble jar sat, and ushered Francis to join her. Each week it would start off empty, but when a child did something suitably impressive, they would get to choose one of the colourful glass spheres and put it in. Francis smiled, cautiously, selecting a yellow and blue one and gently dropping it in.

Nisha and Chrissie were on duty together that lunchtime, and discussed their success as they strode around the playground with their respective hot drinks.

"Do you still not drink coffee?" asked Nisha. Chrissie smiled. She recalled Nisha working hard to acquire the taste while they were revising back when they were eighteen.

"I try and avoid caffeine where I can," she said, lightly.

"You are still a hippy then," said Nisha, gently jabbing Chrissie with her elbow.

Chrissie frowned slightly. The word 'hippy' had become intertwined with some of the accusations her ex-wife had made towards Infinite Bliss. Accusations she had rejected at the time, but which now made perfect sense. She thought of Kiera in that moment, and hoped she knew how sorry she was. For everything. "I just like to know where I am in my body," said Chrissie. "Call me a hippy if you like." She tried not to sound stiff, but could hear the defensive note in her voice. "But I can recommend vanilla chai," she added, attempting to soften things. "It's gorgeous."

"I can smell it from here, so I'll take your word for it," said Nisha, taking a slurp of the instant coffee that Chrissie had spotted her putting two sugars into. "You've changed, though."

"It's been over twenty years," said Chrissie, "of course I've changed."

"Ouch," said Nisha. "Sorry, I didn't mean to upset you."

"No, I'm sorry. It's not your fault." Chrissie sighed. "I mean, I have changed. But probably more in the last couple of years than anything else."

"Sounds like there's a story there," said Nisha. She looked over at Chrissie, and there was a softness in her brown eyes that captured Chrissie for a moment. Memories of that look came flooding back, and a warmth seeped into her body. Chrissie opened her mouth to speak, but Nisha got in first. "But I can see that you don't want to talk about it right now. I understand." They walked on in silence.

After another lap of the playground, Chrissie looked at Nisha and burst into laughter. Nisha looked at her quizzically. "Oh my God, you're still wearing that beret!" said Chrissie.

"Ha! I'd totally forgotten." Nisha reached her hand up to her headwear. "Oh God, so that means when I was telling Hardev to pipe down for the twenty-seventh time, and using my very serious voice – that's trademarked by the way – I was wearing this?"

Chrissie sniggered. "You totally were, Mademoiselle Rajan!"

"Well, merci for that. You should have told me," she said, nudging Chrissie again, who was suddenly feeling more relaxed.

"I think I stopped noticing it, too," Chrissie told her, stopping before she added that she had been looking at how cute Nisha's dimple was when she spoke French, and that it had distracted her. "By the way, I think you did a great job of remembering your dim and distant French degree."

"Well, it's a little more than that. I lived out there for a bit, actually," said Nisha.

Twenty years really was a long time. Chrissie didn't know what she thought Nisha had been doing since they'd last met, but it wasn't living in France – or becoming a teacher, for that matter.

"Oh, really?" said Chrissie. Nisha was eyeing her in a strange way. Chrissie looked back at her, realising they'd both paused in their lap of the playground.

"There's a lot you don't know about me," said Nisha, almost under her breath. Chrissie faltered, and then turned as she heard a scream from behind her.

"Miss!" came an urgent voice. "He's cracked his head open, come quickly!"

Chrissie dashed over towards the child on the ground, Nisha alongside her and a crowd of other children following close behind, desperate to soak up the drama.

"God, I hate blood," said Nisha as they approached.

"It's ok, I'm the first aider on duty, I'll sort it," said Chrissie, striding ahead.

The child on the ground had a small graze. There was blood, but nothing that wouldn't be sorted by the judicious application of a piece of wet blue paper roll – infamous in primary schools for its healing properties. A few minutes later, the ginger-haired boy from Year Three was sitting on a chair in a classroom being tended to by Chrissie.

"I think I need a plaster, Miss," he said.

"I think you'll be fine, Ted. Look, it's stopped bleeding now. I think you can be brave and get on with your day now."

"Yes," said Ted, "perhaps I can." He paused. "I think I'd better take another paper towel though, just in case."

Chrissie nodded, a grave expression on her face. "Well yes, of course Ted, we need to be prepared for any eventuality, including haemorrhage."

Ted nodded back at her, equally serious. Chrissie smiled at him, while writing out a note to hand to his mum later that day. They always had to report any knocks or scrapes, however minor.

Chrissie and Nisha were packing up after the children had gone home for the day. "I think that went ok, don't you?" Nisha commented. "I feel like we're getting into a rhythm with these little guys."

"Honestly, Nisha, they adore you," said Chrissie, wondering why saying those words made her cheeks warm.

"Oh, you're sweet," said Nisha, who seemed wrong-footed for a moment. The dimple appeared.

"Maybe we should grab that drink we talked about," suggested Chrissie, without thinking.

"Oh, I can't," Nisha replied immediately, and Chrissie

felt daft for bringing it up. She should have known that Nisha was just being polite at the start of term.

"No, of course, you have your stuff," said Chrissie, unsure of what she was saying or why, just wanting to fill the awkward silence.

"I just mean, I can't tonight. I have football," said Nisha, who seemed a bit flustered. She was gathering bits and pieces from her desk.

"You still play?" asked Chrissie, grateful for the opportunity to change the subject.

"Yep. Right," said Nisha, "see you tomorrow." She disappeared so quickly that by the time she was gone, Chrissie hadn't even put her coat on.

She sighed to herself. Nisha running out on her. Some things changed. Some things didn't.

Chapter Eight

C hrissie opened her journal. She had time to jot a few things down before meeting Rae at the community centre.

Rule one progress: Nisha. Obviously, I'm not in love with her. Is this an echo of love? Like the memory of a moment? I mean, what even happened back then? No, this is just a frisson of a shadow of a hint of something long dead. We've both lived our own lives since then. And even if I was in love with her (which I'm not), she definitely isn't in love with me, and anyhow, I am not doing this again. Bad things happen when I fall in love.

Rule two progress: No questionable facts believed today, and no cults joined today. Hurrah!

Rule three progress: Off to serve lunch to anyone who needs it today. I'm not changing the world, I get it, but perhaps someone gets a meal today that will keep them going.

Chrissie laid down the glittery pink pen and smiled. Yes. It was all coming along nicely. Rebuilding your life after escaping a cult wasn't easy, but she could do it. She remembered the words of the counsellor she'd seen for the first seven or eight months after she left: *progress isn't always a straight line*. She'd definitely had her jagged moments, but right now she couldn't complain.

She walked the ten minutes to the village square, passing trees as she went. The sun was shining and the leaves were mostly green, but a few were beginning to turn yellow around the edges. Autumn was definitely making its presence felt. She quickly crossed the road before passing the Jam Pot café. She never went in there, preferring the Vine and other cafes.

"Morning," she said, as she walked into the community café attached to the church. Initially Chrissie had been hesitant to join in any activity that might be connected to the church – in the spirit of questioning everything. At first, she'd been concerned that the friendly reverend might try to entice her into the pews. But Rebecca, the vicar, hadn't said a word about prayers or hymns or soul-saving. She'd not tried to offer Chrissie any answers. She simply got on with cooking up massive vats of hearty soup and provided a kind ear for the many people in the area who needed one.

"Morning, bab," said Rebecca, whose warm and rasping Brummie accent was the inevitable result of sixty years in the UK's second city, alongside twenty cigarettes a day.

"Morning, Rebecca. You ok? Shall I sort out the bowls and stuff?"

"Rae's already onto that, but I am sure they'd appreciate your help," said Rebecca, who was somehow buttering multiple slices of bread at the same time as making vast quantities of soup.

"Roger," said Chrissie.

"Morning, lovely," said Rae. "I missed you at yoga yesterday."

"Yeah, sorry about that. We had a meeting that ran late. The last thing I needed!"

"No need to sweat it. I hope you're taking it a bit easier today, though. It is Saturday, after all!"

"You know me," said Chrissie, "I like to keep busy."

"I know, but you need to stop sometimes," Rae replied, a serious expression on their face.

Chrissie didn't answer immediately, feigning interest in the cutlery drawer. She didn't want to have this conversation again. Stopping was scary. She wasn't sure what might happen if she did. The closest she got to stopping was in Rae's yoga class.

"I know, I do," she said, before changing the subject to the new restaurant that had opened up on the high street. Rae raised an eyebrow, but said no more.

"Ready?" said Rebecca, who had left the soup to bubble away and the mountain of buttered bread under copious amounts of cling-film. Chrissie sighed; she'd tried so many times to get Rebecca to abandon cling-film in favour of a more environmentally-friendly reusable covering. "Don't give me that look, bab," said Rebecca, adjusting her bright yellow apron. "I know you think I am single-handedly destroying the planet, but it's the most sanitary way to do it."

"I said nothing," said Chrissie, with a small smile.

"Mmm hmm. You didn't have to. Now then, let's get cracking."

It was almost a repeat of breakfast club at school, with a

diverse group of people – this time adults as well as children – arriving for their meal. They paid what they could, and many of them couldn't pay at all, which was fine.

The chatter in the room made Chrissie feel warm inside. This was so much better than the hungry days she'd endured herself. Hers weren't due to poverty, but rather down to disastrous judgement and decision-making. She recalled the cold, empty days in a Welsh cabin with the others, abandoned by a man Chrissie could now see had been abusing them all along. The charismatic, benevolent leader who'd turned out to be anything but.

Lucian had left them without food or supplies for days on end, in order to 'test their faith'. She thought back to the darkness and despair that had enveloped her, and how she tried to wrangle her brain into believing this was a good thing. She knew now, through hours of counselling, that it had never been a good thing. It was control, coercion and abuse. She looked at Rebecca, the community minded cling-film warrior, making people's lives better, one fag at a time. Never once had she mentioned her faith to Chrissie, but it was clear how she tried to live it – in the service of others. There was no talk of tests, or of faith through suffering. There was enough of that in the world without adding to it deliberately.

She often found herself watching the portly older woman with admiration. Rebecca never sought plaudits or power. She just did her thing. Maybe the planet wouldn't thank her for the added plastic, but Chrissie was sure the people she helped would.

"Hiya," said a voice, rousing Chrissie from her musing.

"Nisha!" she said, in slightly more shocked a voice than she would have liked. Nisha wore her hair in a ponytail and was dressed in a football shirt, shorts and muddy shinpads that poked over a pair of equally-muddy socks. There was a sheen of sweat on her forehead which made Chrissie wonder how warm the teacher was underneath. She shook herself slightly. No.

"Yep, that's right. Nothing wrong with your vision today," said Nisha, grinning and appearing much more relaxed than she had in the week.

"Been playing football?" asked Chrissie.

"You don't miss a trick do you?" said Nisha, with a warmth alongside the teasing. Chrissie laughed, her cheeks going pink. "Yeah, I've joined a local women's team and there was an informal kickabout in Kings Heath Park earlier. I thought I'd come and get some soup – if it's still going?"

"Everyone's welcome," said Chrissie, and served Nisha a generous bowl with a couple of slices of bread. Nisha dropped a tenner into the bowl. "It's quietened down a bit. I'll come and join you," she said, before she could stop herself.

"Great," said Nisha. There was that grin again. And the dimple.

Oh, the dimple!

Chrissie walked over, trying to silence the voice in her head that had started bellowing out "Oh, Ms Rajan's dimple" to the tune of Seven Nation Army. She needed her journal, and she needed it the moment she got home.

"I'm just popping out for a fag, Chrissie," said the vicar, sweeping past clutching a packet of Silk Cut. Chrissie smiled and waved, knowing that during the course of her cigarette break, Rebecca would end up chatting to a few hungry or lonely souls and bringing them back in for soup and bread.

"So, tell me, what's been happening with you in the last

twenty years? I mean, it'll have to be the edited highlights, as I need to go to Holland and Barratt in a bit," said Chrissie.

"Touche," replied Nisha. "Well, I went to uni and studied French and Maths."

"I remember that," said Chrissie. "UCL, right?"

"Yeah, London. I spent a bit of time in France as part of that, and went back after my course as well."

"Ooh la la, Ms Rajan, très, um, exciting," said Chrissie, her GCSE French letting her down.

"It looks to me like you need those lessons as much as the children do. Yeah, I was in Paris for a bit, which was amazing." Nisha took a mouthful of soup. "In fact, I was wondering if we could take the kids to Paris for a short school trip? It would be an amazing way for them to try out their new skills."

"Oh my God," said Chrissie, "that would be awesome! Some of those children have never been outside Birmingham, let alone the UK."

"Well, I know for a fact that Dottie went to Disney Land last year," replied Nisha, her eyes sparkling.

"Oh my, don't we all know about that! If I had a pound for every time she mentioned it…" Chrissie tailed off.

"But yeah, I think we could make it work. Do you reckon Dan would come with? The three of us could do it, right? It's a small class group."

Nisha and Dan seemed to have struck up quite the friendship since the start of term. Chrissie wasn't sure about how she felt about it. But she knew she couldn't control it.

"I'm sure he would," said Chrissie. "But back to your life in France," she pressed, curious to know what had happened next.

"So I worked there for a bit, and I met someone. Someone I fell in love with."

Chrissie's heart began to beat inexplicably quickly. "Someone?"

"Jake. We were working in a bar together and when we met, we didn't really look back."

"French?" asked Chrissie, processing the male name, her brain working overtime. Nisha was straight. Yes. Of course she was. Why shouldn't she be? And anyway, it didn't matter, right?

"No, from London. In fact, we both moved back to London and lived together there. We both trained as teachers, and that's where I've been ever since. I was teaching in an inner-city primary school."

"And this, um Jake," said Chrissie, the name jagged in her mouth. "He's in Birmingham with you?"

Nisha's face clouded. "No. We split up a few months ago. It was all quite difficult."

Seeing her friend's obvious sadness, Chrissie's empathy pushed everything else aside. She reached her hand out and rested it on Nisha's arm. Nisha looked up at her, surprised at the physical contact. "I'm sorry, that sounds really hard," said Chrissie.

"Mmm, yeah, it was." Nisha wiped the final remnants of the soup from her bowl with a crust. "But it was for the best in the end. We'd grown apart. I think we both needed to admit to ourselves that it was time to move on. It just took us a little while."

"So that's why you came back home to Birmingham?" asked Chrissie.

"Partly. Jake and I taught in the same school. While we parted on amicable terms, it felt weird to carry on working together every day. I decided I needed a fresh start, and I saw all the gorgeous pictures and film of Birmingham during the Commonwealth Games in 2022, and I thought, well, it's as good a place as any. I have history here."

Chrissie nodded. Yes. History. "It sounds like you made a good job of a very difficult situation. It must have been hard," she said again.

"Yeah. I guess." Nisha screwed up her face momentarily. She looked like she wanted to say something else, but quickly moved on. "Anyway, enough about me. What about you?" asked Nisha, leaning towards Chrissie. "I'm guessing you haven't spent the last twenty years doing nothing."

"Well, no," said Chrissie, wondering where to start. "I went to uni, obviously."

"You were going to do psychology at Leicester, right?"

"Yeah. That's what I did. And I've done all sorts of jobs since then." Chrissie faltered. She didn't have any tales of Paris or exotic travel. She'd come home after university and moved back in with her dad.

"But you came back to Brum? To be close to Don?"

Chrissie smiled, enjoying hearing his name. "Yeah, to be with Dad."

"How is he?" asked Nisha. "He was always so lovely – didn't seem to mind us camping out in the garden that summer."

There was a pause in the conversation. It was the first time either of them had acknowledged that summer. They had mostly stuck to work talk, or small talk. Hearing Nisha mention it made Chrissie shiver, slightly. Would they have to go over that? She wasn't sure she wanted to. But there was something else, too, a sadness she had to share.

Chrissie set her face and broke it to Nisha as gently as she could. "He died, eight years ago."

Nisha's face fell. "Oh, Chris, I'm so sorry," she said, wrapping her fingers around Chrissie's wrist.

"It was a long time ago," said Chrissie, ignoring the tears that welled up in her eyes. It seemed forever since she'd spoken to anyone who knew Don. There was something evocative and painful about it, but at the same time, something welcome. "He'd been ill for so long. I was with him." She looked at Nisha, whose own eyes had started to fill.

"I'm so sorry. And I wasn't here." She squeezed Chrissie's hand. "I'm sorry I disappeared on you. You deserved so much better than that."

"Well, Nish," said Chrissie, using the nickname she'd not spoken in two decades, "that was a very long time ago. We've both moved on since then." But somewhere in her heart she felt something change. Nisha had never explained what had happened before, and much less said sorry. She'd spent years dreaming of Nisha coming back and saying sorry. And here she was.

But everything was different now.

Nisha's face clouded. "You seem so put together, so sure of yourself. I'm glad you had such strength through all that." Chrissie nodded, absentmindedly, trying to ignore the warmth that travelled up her arm from Nisha's fingers now tangled with her own.

"I had help," said Chrissie, before excusing herself to help with the clearing up.

Chapter Nine

Early morning yoga on a Monday was one of the rare occasions where Dan would join Chrissie and Rae. Seven am in the community centre with fellow early risers was the perfect way to start the week.

Rae was wearing their customary baggy shorts and fitted vest top, while Chrissie preferred her tie-die T-shirt and leggings. Dan, however, was wearing his school issue tracksuit as his class had PE on Mondays.

The class was coming to an end. Rae's gentle voice slowly brought the group from their peaceful prone position in shavasana. "And gently bring your awareness to your fingertips, your toes, your head."

Chrissie flicked her eyes open and began to make small movements. "That's right," said Rae, their voice still low. "Slowly bring yourself up into a sitting position."

The class began to rouse from the pose that served as the reward at the end of a long and strenuous yoga class.

"Bring your hands together, thumbs to your forehead,"

said Rae and the class did as they were told. "Namaste," Rae added.

"Namaste," said Chrissie softly. It was something she hadn't been able to say when she'd first started. Not until she'd researched the origin of the word, which in this context was about bowing to oneself; thanking yourself for taking care of your body. In many ways, yoga was the only healthy vestige of Infinite Bliss. She was grateful to still have it as an outlet. It was a way of bringing her body and mind together and being at one with the world.

"I think it's my turn to get the coffees," said Dan, as they strolled along the high street towards school.

"Well, I won't complain. Although obviously it'll be a chai latte for me, please," said Chrissie.

"Obviously," replied Dan. The coffee shop at the top of the high street had only just opened, and they were served quickly. Chrissie had remembered to bring reusable take-away cups. Dan always forgot, so she tended to bring one for him too.

"So, how're things going with your old friend?" asked Dan, as they continued their journey to work. "She seems pretty sound."

"Yes, she is. The kids love her." Chrissie smiled.

"Did you know her well back in the day? I mean, I know you said you were friends and there was a bust-up," asked Dan, clearly desperate to find out the back story, in spite of his earlier attempt not to pry. "Were you just friends?" he said, giving her a nudge. Chrissie took a sip of her too-hot drink to buy time to work out what to say. "I had a 'best friend' at high school too," continued Dan, "and I can tell you, she and I were *very* friendly," he added, with a grin. They left the café and began to walk towards the school.

"Oh, it's far too early to hear about your teenage shenanigans," said Chrissie.

"Ah, it wasn't like that," Dan replied. "It was actually very sweet. She was my first love."

"Bless you. That sounds lovely," said Chrissie. She could imagine Dan would have been a very sweet first boyfriend for the right girl.

"We went to different unis, and the whole distance thing didn't work out. But we stayed friends. She's married to a stockbroker now, I think. Perhaps she's traded up?" he said, blowing on his drink.

"From you, Mr Harvey, never," Chrissie insisted.

"But don't change the subject. What are we talking here with Nisha – best friends, experimentation, first love?" Dan's red hair flopped over his brown eyes, which felt like they were piercing Chrissie's soul. She didn't know what to say. All of the above? None of the above?

Always questioning.

"Oh my," said Dan, "you had a thing with her, didn't you? I was only joking, but this really was a thing." He rubbed his hands together in glee.

"Ugh," said Chrissie. "Ok, yes, there was a thing. But saying it was a 'thing' makes it sound tawdry, which it absolutely was not." There was an edge to her voice that made Dan raise his eyebrows.

"Sorry, bab, I didn't meant to upset you," he said, concern laced through his eyes.

"No, I'm sorry. I didn't mean to snap. Yes, it was a thing. A big thing. A big thing that ended badly."

"Teenage love is hard, right? Believe me, I remember." They were walking in through the school gates now. "Look, you don't have to tell me about it, but if you ever want to, you know where I am."

"Ta, love. In the meantime, has Nisha told you about her plans for a trip to France?" Chrissie was relieved to change the subject. She wasn't sure how best to describe her current situation. The journal was calling.

Chapter Ten

"How about the Jam Pot?" asked Nisha. It was lunchtime in the staffroom and she was outlining her school trip master plan to Dan and Chrissie. They'd agreed to meet up to discuss it after work, and Nisha was suggesting the café on the high street.

"Ah," said Chrissie, looking beseechingly at Dan.

"We don't go to the Jam Pot," said Dan. He lowered his voice. "Well, at least Chrissie doesn't."

Nisha furrowed her brow. "Er, why? Do you have some kind of coffee and toast aversion?"

"Well, I don't do coffee, as you know," Chrissie reminded her, setting her hands on her thighs and readying herself for what was next. "And I am trying to reduce my wheat intake."

Dan rolled his eyes. "But that's not why, though, is it?"

Chrissie sighed. Nisha was watching carefully, her eyes moving from Dan to Chrissie and back like she was watching a tennis match. "No. That's not why. So," she said, pausing to take a breath, "my ex-wife's partner runs the café."

Nisha flushed very slightly, which struck Chrissie as a little odd. But she carried on speaking. "We divorced a couple of years ago. It was a bit messy. Her new partner seems lovely. But it would be weird to go inside."

"Wheat content notwithstanding," said Dan, patting Chrissie's knee. "Seymour, the woman who runs the place, is actually very sweet. But Chrissie and I tend to favour the Vine."

Nisha didn't say anything for a moment, so Dan filled the gap. "The bonus is that the Vine serve alcoholic drinks as well."

"Well, count me in," said Nisha, as though the previous conversation hadn't happened. Chrissie wondered whether it had triggered thoughts of her own separation with Jake. But before she could consider probing any further, the bell went and the three agreed to pick up where they'd left off at the café bar.

By the time they'd had a couple of drinks – Nisha on beer, Dan on rum and coke and Chrissie on white wine –the whole plan had been put together. They would go to Paris with the class for three nights and show them the sights. They'd go by coach and travel on Le Shuttle.

"Oh my goodness, I'm so excited," said Nisha. "I never got to do anything this cool when I was in primary school. They're going to love it."

"You bet they are," replied Chrissie. "I can just see it now. We'll be drifting down the Champs-Elysees, showing them the Arc de Triumph, the Eiffel Tower and how amazing it is to be able to speak another language."

"Right," said Dan, "much as I'm with you on all this,

firstly, we will have a class of kids with us. They will be less drifting down the Champs-Elysees than creating chaos at every step, and you know it. It will be hard work. You must know that." He paused and sipped his drink.

Nisha giggled. She said: "But it will be fun chaos. School trips are the happiest of all my school memories. I always loved a sleepover." She locked eyes with Chrissie briefly, before looking away. Chrissie felt her heart pound in her chest for reasons she chose not to think about.

"But secondly," said Dan, "what about the cash? Some of these kids have literally nothing at home. Their only proper meals all week come from the school kitchen. I know some of the families will be able to pay, but what about the others?"

"It's a good point," said Nisha with a frown.

"I think if we do this, we need to make sure every child can come, if they want to," Chrissie added. This was what her life was about now, making good things happen for others.

They all fell silent, and took the opportunity to take sips of their drinks. Nisha spoke first. "Well, when my footy team in London went to a tournament in Europe a couple of years back, we managed to get a local company to sponsor us to bring the costs down. This would be a much smaller undertaking. Maybe we should see if anyone's willing to sponsor us?"

"Yes," said Chrissie, feeling the energy surging through her. "That's it, we can get a sponsor. And I know just the person to ask for help."

"Well, you two ladies seem to have it all sewn up," said Dan.

"We're women, thank you very much," replied Nisha, a

faux frown on her face. She smiled. "But yes, we're all over it."

"Excellent," he said. "I have marking to do. I'll see you both tomorrow."

He gathered his things, kissed them both on the cheek, and then left.

"Another drink, my lady?" asked Chrissie, emboldened by the wine.

"Ugh, you can stop with that, I'm not Penelope Featherington, and you're not Colin Bridgerton!" They both laughed. "But yes, I'll have another of these." She waved the almost empty branded beer glass she was holding.

By the time Chrissie had returned to the table, and the overhead lighting had been turned down, and a member of staff had put a lit tealight in a jar between them, the bar was definitely on evening mode. "Aha, thanks," said Nisha. She gestured to the room and spoke again: "It would seem that romance is on the agenda."

"I, er, well, I mean." Chrissie fumbled with her words, her hands shaking as she put the drinks down. Had she missed an episode?

"They obviously think so here," continued Nisha, grinning her most winning smile. "Check out the candles on all the tables. And isn't that Lionel Richie coming through the speakers now? Old school."

"Very old school," said Chrissie, relieved they had moved on from her stumbling faux pas. Of course Nisha didn't mean they were having a romantic moment. Of course not. If Chrissie knew anything about the modern-day Nisha, it was that she was probably straight. She needed to have a word with her runaway imagination.

"Do you mind if I ask you something?" asked Nisha, her

strong arm holding her pint to her lips as she finished speaking.

"I suppose not," said Chrissie, holding her breath and wondering where the heck this was heading.

"What happened with your marriage?"

Chrissie let out the breath she'd been holding. "What happened?" she sighed. "I wrecked it."

Chapter Eleven

I t wasn't a story she told often, nor was it one she was proud of, but it was part of who she was and she knew she had to own it. She was terrified Nisha might judge her for it, but she went ahead anyway.

The two of them went back too far for her to pretend.

"We met not long after Dad died. Kiera lived near me – still does. She works at the hospital. Anyway, she was this wonderful, sensible, kind person who came into my life at absolutely the perfect time. I'm not sure how I would have coped in the years that followed his death without her."

Nisha nodded, saying nothing. Chrissie continued. "It was wonderful, it really was. We worked so well together. But life was hard. I struggled to find meaning in anything. Things started to change for the better for me when I discovered Infinite Bliss."

"Infinite Bliss? Is that new age hippy stuff?" asked Nisha.

"Yes," said Chrissie, exhaling before she went on. "Well, that's how they described themselves. I would go to these wonderful workshops where I'd get in touch with my inner soul, where the world would be explained to me, and meaning derived from everything from plants to food to movement. Kiera hated it. She thought they were charlatans." She paused on that. Ultimately, Kiera had been right. "She dismissed them out of hand. And it only pushed me further in, if I'm honest. I found myself doing something with the community almost every night. And we'd go on these amazing residentials over long weekends. It was like I'd come home. The leader, Lucian, he could explain everything – why the world was the way it was, how we could make it better, how we could reach enlightenment."

"Sounds sketchy," said Nisha.

Chrissie frowned. "In retrospect, yes. But at the time it felt like suddenly everything made sense. The more I got involved, the better my life got, or so I thought. But also, the further I got from my wife. She turned from the kind, thoughtful person I'd married into someone who was always suspicious of the people I spent time with, and increasingly angry and agitated with me. I mean, I sort of get that now. I think she was trying to protect me – to protect herself too. But at the time, it just drove an even greater wedge between us."

"Confirmation bias," said Nisha, absently.

"What?"

"Confirmation bias – basically, you wanted to believe what this bloke was telling you, and so you did. Kiera disagreed, but rather than bringing you round to her viewpoint, you ended up moving further away," said Nisha.

"I guess so," agreed Chrissie. "But it really wasn't her fault. I had a lot of therapy after I came out of Infinite Bliss, and I now realise that so much of what happened was my doing and my responsibility."

Chrissie continued to relate the slow deterioration of her marriage, the way Lucian had encouraged members only to have relationships with those in the group – those who had reached the same plane of enlightenment. The way he'd encouraged polyamory. By this point, Chrissie was utterly under his spell.

"How old was he?" asked Nisha at one point.

"Er, in his mid to late sixties, I think," said Chrissie, picturing the charismatic man with white hair.

"Same age as your dad would have been," said Nisha. Chrissie gave a rueful smile. This was something she had explored with her counsellor. Lucian had become a paternal figure to many of them, but with the recent death of her own father, it was all the more potent for Chrissie.

"Yes. And I craved his approval. I can't explain to you the power he had over me. Over all of us. There was a small group of us, and it was like we were the chosen ones. He'd talk about how far we'd transcended western materialism, and that others in the group should look to us for inspiration. It was a heady mix of approval and worship."

Nisha nodded. "Wow." They sat quietly without speaking for a moment. "So, you left your wife?"

"I guess it would be more accurate to say she left me, but I am not sure I left her much choice. I was already seeing Athena by then, and had fully embraced the idea that polyamory was the way forward," said Chrissie. "And Lucian was encouraging us all to break our 'worldly bonds' as he called them." She used her fingers to signify speech marks. "Essentially, I dumped her, but tried to suggest it was her fault. She left and had to find somewhere else to live."

Chrissie felt a tear drop down her face. Saying the words out loud to Nisha brought it all back. And she couldn't help but wonder if Nisha would judge her for it, think less of her, not want to have anything to do with her.

She wouldn't be the only one.

Nisha stood up. Chrissie looked down. Of course, Nisha would leave now. It was really only to be expected. She still felt shame for all she had done, and she couldn't undo anything. But it was hard to experience another person choosing to break off contact with her. Although how they would manage that at work, Chrissie didn't know. She hoped she wouldn't have to resign.

To her surprise, she felt movement beside her and looked up. Nisha had moved round the table so she was sitting next to Chrissie. "It's ok," she whispered as she put an arm around Chrissie's shoulders.

Chrissie shuddered at the contact, shocked and relieved. "It's not ok. It was never ok. But I have acknowledged that. I have said sorry to Kiera and made all the amends I can – including repaying her money that Lucian persuaded me to give Infinite Bliss." She covered her face, not wanting to see Nisha's inevitable disappointment with her. "I know, it's appalling. I stole money that was ours. Honestly, I'm a truly despicable person."

"You're not, Chris," said Nisha.

No one had called Chrissie that since Nisha herself, back at school.

"Yeah," she continued. "You've done some seriously questionable things, but it sounds like you've done all you can to learn from the experience and put things right. And, you know, I wonder if you were a victim yourself? It sounds like this bloke was a proper wrong-un. You were grieving." Nisha squeezed Chrissie's shoulder and took a few big mouthfuls of beer.

"I was. But I feel like I have to own what I did, whatever

the reasons were. I will spend the rest of my life trying to make it ok. That's why I have three rules I live by," said Chrissie, pulling herself back together.

"Three rules," said Nisha. "Ok, let's hear them. I've not done such a great job with my life, so maybe I should adopt them too."

Chrissie laughed. "This is my own personal journey. If you want rules, you have to make your own."

Nisha smiled before she spoke: "I see you haven't fully abandoned the hippy life."

"I will always be me," she said, quietly. "Ok, you ready?" Nisha nodded. "Rule one: don't fall in love. Rule two: question everything. A lot of the trouble I got into before was because I didn't question the information I was being given. I was being lied to every day and I can never let that happen again. And rule three: give back. That's how I ended up working at the school, why I volunteer at the community centre and all that stuff. I want to make amends."

"Ok," said Nisha. "I get rules two and three. Arguably, I think those are rules we can all live by. But why are you saying you can't fall in love? What the hell is that about?" She was slurring her words slightly.

Chrissie felt annoyance rise inside her. She hadn't shared this with many people, and Nisha's disdain hurt. She felt it sharply in her chest. "You've had too much to drink," she said, shortly.

"You've had the same amount as me," Nisha pointed out. "And you're trying to change the subject. I mean it, what the hell is going on with you? Don't you think you deserve happiness like everyone else?" Her voice was rising. "Or do you want to be some kind of saint?"

"I'm no saint," said Chrissie, her voice coming out

louder than she had planned. She felt like the walls of the café bar were closing in on her. Her breaths came fast. "You've heard how far from sainthood I am."

"But you seem to want to be one, with this mad vow of celibacy," said Nisha, gesticulating wildly.

"I don't think we should talk about this anymore," Chrissie told her.

"But I want to know what this is about," said Nisha, her mouth now a straight line.

Chrissie shifted so she wasn't so close to her colleague. She reached for her jacket. "I've already told you. And I don't understand why you're so interested," she added. "It's not like I've heard from you in more than twenty years."

"Wow, ok, so we're going there, are we?" Nisha said with a frown.

"Look, I'm going to go." Before Nisha could say anything more, Chrissie walked briskly out of the bar without looking back, the words they'd just exchanged spinning in her head.

Chapter Twelve

Chrissie held her journal, hugging it tight. It had been a while since she'd written about her father. Don had been a warm, friendly sort of guy, and loved Chrissie with all his heart. Her mother had left when she was young, and he had raised her alone. Despite her mum's absence, she had never felt much of a gap – her memories of her were vague at best. But Don had been an evergreen presence in her life.

During her teens he had become unwell, and she had spent a lot of time looking after him. Most often they'd watch TV together, or perhaps read. He never expected her to care for him, but it was a labour of love for Chrissie. She remembered him peering over his half-moon reading glasses at her, his balding head shaking as she talked about horoscopes or new age philosophy. He hadn't been a fan. But he'd taken her interests in good humour, reminding her at all times: "Remember who you are, Christina Anderson, you are the one and only daughter of Don Anderson, and that counts for something."

At the time, Chrissie hadn't understood what he meant. Perhaps she was beginning to now. He'd have hated Lucian and the Infinite Bliss group. He'd never have understood. But somewhere along the lines she had lost herself. Maybe she'd shamed his memory.

Don had loved Nisha and happily tolerated the two of them camping out in the back garden in his old tent after their exams were over. He said it made the house nice and peaceful and left them to it. He'd comforted Chrissie the day Nisha left, even though he didn't really understand what was going on. Chrissie didn't feel she could tell him at the time. Looking back, she wondered if he had guessed.

Chrissie smiled to herself. It was nice to think about him now. There would always be pain there, but there was a sweetness too, an echo of the unconditional love he'd always shown her. She wondered what he would think of her rules. She sighed. He'd probably have lit his pipe and declared: "Poppycock, bab." There would have been a kindness to it, but he'd have dismissed it regardless. He always seemed to know exactly who he was and what he was doing.

But it couldn't always have been that way. Somewhere along the lines his life had undergone radical change, when Chrissie's mum ran out on them both. He'd never spoken ill of her, something Chrissie was grateful for. Whatever else the woman was, she was Chrissie's mother, and someone he had loved once.

Over the years, people had asked her if she wanted to track her mother down. She knew she didn't. Giving birth to someone didn't give them automatic right of entry to your life. Chrissie could have walked past her mum in the street for all she knew. But then again, had she had a responsible parent around, perhaps she wouldn't have turned her whole life upside down – and dragged Kiera's along with it. Don certainly wouldn't have let that happen. But Don was gone by the time she met Kiera.

Chrissie put the journal down on her desk and went into the kitchen. She gathered her possessions and headed out into the world. She had to get to school. She was dreading seeing Nisha again after the night before. It was rare for her to walk off in a strop, but somewhere between their history and Nisha's needling, she'd been pushed too far.

She walked along the high street. It was still early, and the only place that was open was the Jam Pot. She risked a peep inside. She didn't recognise the woman at the counter, so for once she took a chance and went in. The café really did the best toast in Kings Heath. She ordered herself a chai latte and some brown toast with almond butter on to take into school with her. She hoped it would embolden her for the inevitable awkward morning with Nisha.

Nisha was already in the classroom as she arrived, and much to Chrissie's surprise, she was beaming her warmest smile at her teaching assistant. "Morning, Chrissie," said Nisha.

"Morning," replied Chrissie, confused, but at least pleased not to walk into a continuation of last night's conversation.

"Ah, good morning, Miss Anderson," added Mrs Hemingway, who was sitting behind Nisha. As Chrissie examined her old friend's flawless face more closely, she noticed that her eyes seemed slightly wild.

"Good morning, Mrs Hemingway," said Chrissie lightly. "To what do we owe this pleasure?"

"I've been hearing all about your proposed trip to Paris with your class." Her face was unreadable, but instinctively Chrissie felt that this was not good. She smiled her most winning smile. "I must tell you," Mrs Hemingway continued, "that I have grave doubts about running this kind of trip with such young children. You'd be a long way from the school, and a very long way from their parents."

Chrissie looked over at Nisha, who swallowed, but said nothing. Mrs Hemingway carried on. "And while I understand your desire to raise the aspirations of some of our youngsters, I'm not sure this is the way. Aside from anything else, some of the children's families wouldn't be in any position to pay for such a lavish trip."

Nisha frowned, seemingly lost for words. Chrissie knew that if she didn't speak now, this trip was dead in the water. And for some reason it felt very important not to let that happen, especially after their conversation last night. "I completely understand where you're coming from," she said, "and I share some of your concerns." She side-eyed Nisha, trying to reassure her that she had a plan. "But I do wonder whether, if we can manage all of the risks you've rightly mentioned, this might actually be formative for the children in this class?"

Both Chrissie and Nisha's eyes were on Mrs Hemingway. The head teacher emitted no sound or expression. "It could even help some of them build resilience and confidence," said Nisha, finding her voice. "Mr Harvey is up for helping, and Chrissie has some routes into funding."

Chrissie noted that Nisha didn't look at her while she spoke. They both knew full well that she had yet to secure any funding at all. She pursed her lips. Mrs Hemingway didn't need to know this, but it wasn't a problem they could explain away for any length of time without a real cash injection.

"Perhaps," continued Nisha, warming to her theme, "this is how we help make their learning make more sense to them? We could gear the curriculum towards all things

Paris – Maths about the Eiffel Tower, Geography about France, History about the musketeers."

There was a silence that went on for a good ten seconds, during which time Chrissie decided that they were about to be given a solid, gold-plated, 'No'.

"I can see you've thought all of this through," said Mrs Hemingway, rubbing her hands together slowly, her beads clacking as she moved. "I'm impressed." Chrissie and Nisha waited with bated breath. "Ok. You need to make sure you have all the bases covered in the next few weeks, including the cash, if you want permission to do this." Mrs Hemingway looked at the women. "Good luck." She winked and left the room.

Chrissie and Nisha sagged against the classroom tables they were standing by. "Oh my God, you've totally saved us there," said Nisha, fanning her face with her fingers.

"I think it was a team effort," replied Chrissie, unable to keep the smile from her face, even though she was still smarting from their last conversation.

"No, if you hadn't been here, being your eternally positive and optimistic self, I'd have totally caved and agreed it was a terrible idea and we shouldn't do it." Nisha straightened and walked over to the smart board, ready to load it up for the first lesson of the day. She looked over her shoulder at Chrissie. "Thank you." She smiled broadly, her hair falling over her eyes, reminding Chrissie of the young Nisha that Chrissie had known so well. "This isn't a mistake though, is it?" Nisha's brow faltered.

"No," said Chrissie, trying to think only about the school trip, rather than the wisdom of them working together. "I think it's an awesome idea. And I think we're going to pull it off." She tried to make her smile warm, and not like that of a teenager with a crush. Because neither of those things were the case. Obviously. "I have to tell you, though," she added, "I have found literally no funding whatsoever yet. But I am totally on it."

"I don't doubt it," said Nisha. "You're awesome. And about last night," she began, but anything she was about to say was interrupted by a mum banging on the classroom window. Parents were supposed to wait patiently outside the classroom until the door was open, even if they needed to speak to a teacher.

Chrissie whispered, "It's Dottie's mum." Nisha moved her head slightly so she could roll her eyes without being spotted through the window.

"And she appears to be as much of a handful as her darling daughter. Oh, what joy!" Nisha papered a professional smile on her face and headed towards the door. It was nearly time to let the children in, anyway.

Chapter Thirteen

"Dan!" said Nisha, accosting him in the staffroom at lunchtime, Chrissie smirking beside her. "Did you spill the beans?" She pursed her lips at her colleague as he made himself an unfeasibly strong coffee from the kitchen area, and he pulled a confused face in response. "You know what they say," Nisha continued, "snitches get stitches!"

Holding his coffee in his other hand, his mug declaring 'I heart Geography', Dan put his free hand up and backed away. "What have I done?"

Chrissie giggled. "Well, if I may speak for Reggie Kray here, I think you'll find that we had a visit from the boss this morning taking us to task about Paris." Dan's mouth formed a small 'o' shape. "And given that only the three of us knew about it, and neither of us have said anything, it was a process of elimination."

"Ah," said Dan, reddening slightly.

"Yes," said Nisha. "Elementary, dear Watson." She bumped her elbow with Chrissie's, who felt a tingle spread from her arm.

"Yes, sorry. You know what I get like when she's around," he said.

The three walked to their favoured corner of the staff room. "She scares you," said Chrissie.

"Yes," he agreed. "And honestly, if she doesn't scare you, you're missing something. That woman has Jedi skills. I don't even know how I ended up telling her, she just looked at me yesterday after the staff meeting and it all came pouring out."

Nisha rolled her eyes. "Oh, don't worry," said Chrissie, patting his arm. "It was ok. We managed to do some quick thinking and get things back on track."

"Well, Chrissie did," Nisha pointed out with a half smile. "But we have to come up with the goods – a cast iron plan and some cash. Neither of which we have at present."

"Oh, well done," said Dan, "you're both made of sterner stuff than me, clearly."

"Clearly," said Nisha. She grinned. "We're going to have to have a serious think about how we get this organised, though. We need to sort staffing and everything."

"I totally believe we can do it," said Chrissie, a sense of joyous confidence coming over her. "If we really want it to happen, and put our hearts and souls into it, we can."

"Ah, there's the hippy we know and love," replied Nisha, a fond tone in her voice – a tone that felt like it might hold an apology somewhere.

Chrissie laughed. She spoke again. "I'll put my thinking cap on in the next few days, and then perhaps the three of us can meet up and create a masterplan?"

Dan and Nisha nodded. "Oh," said Chrissie, "dare I ask what Dottie's mum wanted?"

"Something tiresome about the PTA. Did you know she's the chair?" asked Nisha.

Dan piped up. "Philippa? Yes, I think she may have mentioned it. A few hundred times."

"Ah," said Nisha, "her reputation goes before her." She opened her lunchbox and took out a floppy cheese sandwich. "She wanted to talk to me about the school festive fete in November."

"I mean," said Dan, "it's a Christmas fete."

"Yes," said Chrissie, "but Philippa is concerned that people of other faiths may be offended by calling it that, so she never calls it that."

Nisha rolled her eyes, "But we mark Diwali and Eid and Passover as well at the school. It's a Christmas fete, everyone knows it!" she sighed. "But that's not what she was talking about. She wants us to do a call-out for stuff to sell at the bring-and-buy stall."

"She doesn't want much, does she?" said Dan. "Is she aware that Ofsted could visit us at any time *and* we have SATs to prepare for?"

"Don't give her such a hard time," Chrissie told him. "She's trying to do what she can for the school. She doesn't have to worry about Ofsted and SATs, and in reality, the kids shouldn't be worried about that either, should they?" Nisha and Dan gave sage nods. "Perhaps we have an opportunity here?"

"What do you mean?" asked Nisha.

"She's chair of the PTA, right?" said Chrissie, furrowing her brow.

"Yes," said Dan, frowning. "I'm not sure where you're going with this."

"So, she'll have all the clearances for working with children and vulnerable people, right?"

"Well, maybe," replied Nisha, suddenly cottoning on.

"Wouldn't she be just the person to help us in our

mission to get Year Four to Paris? She could come too, and help us organise it," said Chrissie.

"Oh my God, you're a genius," said Dan. "She has the organisation skills of an air traffic controller." He paused and thought for a moment before speaking again. "It would mean we'd have to actually spend time with her, though."

"She's not so bad," said Chrissie. "And it might distract her from her quest to turn the 'festive' fete into the event of the season."

Nisha smiled. She looked pleased with the idea, and gave Chrissie a warm look that made her feel slightly liquid inside. She excused herself to go to the toilet. This was going to have to stop. She couldn't keep having such strong a physical reaction to Nisha.

Chapter Fourteen

The weekend came as a welcome relief after a busy few days at work and out of it. Chrissie and Nisha hadn't been able to talk properly alone, and soon a day or two had gone by and they hadn't addressed what had gone between them at the café bar. It was as though it had never happened, swept up in planning for Operation Croissant, as Nisha had started to call it. Not the most subtle of code names.

But for Chrissie, the words Nisha had said kept coming back to her. She sat at her kitchen table, the rain pouring down the window pane, writing in the purple-bound notebook that served as her journal.

"Do I think I deserve happiness?" she wrote. Then below that she added "do I think I am some kind of saint?" She laughed. Of course she didn't. She got out a red pen and wrote "NO" in capital letters under the second question.

She looked again at the first question, seeking the right coloured pen with which to write "yes," but she couldn't find it. It was curious, because she had approximately fifteen pens in various shades of rainbow colours. She left the question unanswered. Something about it made her uncomfortable.

She closed the book and put the pen on top of it. Her empty peppermint tea mug went beside it. She stood and walked to the hallway to put on her coat. It was still raining, but she wanted to get out of her own four walls and away from her thoughts. Rationally, she knew she couldn't escape her thoughts, but somewhere inside, she wondered if the rain might wash her confusion away.

She donned a pair of hot pink wellies and put her hood up before facing the deluge. She headed to Kings Heath Park, only a few minutes' walk away. The playground, usually full of children, was empty and dripping. The grass seemed greener in the rain. Chrissie made for the small woodland area beyond the climbing frame and headed into the trees. The oaks provided limited protection, but there was a sense of escaping from the world amid their branches and leaves. She came upon a large den made of sticks and branches and smiled. She'd loved making dens as a child, imagining fairies and pixies coming to join her. She'd loved reading the *Magical Faraway Tree* stories by Enid Blyton, escaping into a world of fantasy. Her dad had taught her how to use tree trunks for added structural integrity.

She carried on walking, already feeling better for going out. There was something soothing about the sound of the rain on the trees, the squelch of mud beneath her boots and the feel of dampness on her cheeks. She felt more her usual self in this environment, and her reeling thoughts began to quieten.

From the woods she headed down to the bottom of the park, below the old bowling green where on sunny Saturdays people would gather to do tai chi together. There were a few determined dog walkers out, nodding their hellos to Chrissie. There was a sense of camaraderie between those braving the rain this morning.

As she came up the hill and past the Victorian tearooms, she made her way to the more open areas where picnics would take place in sunny weather. There was a group of about ten women playing football, in spite of the rain. They seemed to be having a whale of a time, leaping about, whooping and cheering and embracing the mud and the wet. A goal was scored and everyone cheered, even the opposing side. Chrissie paused to watch for a while. They were all soaked to the skin, but loving it anyway. It made her feel good to see people rejoicing in the downpour.

There was a tall, slim woman, her long ponytail stuck to her back, gloved hands always poised and ready for the ball. She had an impressive reach and kept a surprising number of balls out of the net. But just as it seemed no one would be able to score against her, a small, solid player ran right at her, stuck out her tongue through the hair plastered all over her face, and sent the ball through her legs. The cheers started before the ball even hit the back of the goal, and the woman was besieged by her teammates.

Chrissie laughed. She'd never liked football, but watching this game made her want to join in. "Come on!" came a voice from the pitch, a voice that sounded familiar. The goal-scorer was gesturing to Chrissie. "You know you want to join in," she added, with a grin that was entirely familiar now she'd swept her wet hair away and Chrissie could see her dimpled face properly.

"Nisha!" she exclaimed. "You mad thing! There's no way I'm making a fool of myself with you professionals." Nisha gently jogged over to where Chrissie was standing.

Her hair was dripping, there was mud up to her knees, but her brown eyes shone from her face.

"Tell me you don't fancy having a go." Nisha gave her a wink. "I never managed to persuade you back in the day, but perhaps it's time for something new."

Chrissie pursed her lips. Nisha had played football several times a week when they were at school, forever trying to get Chrissie to join her. Perhaps it was time to take up the offer. "But I don't have the right clothes on." She gestured to her wellies, glowing pink.

"They look pretty ideal to me," said Nisha, motioning to the sodden trainers she was wearing. "Come on," she said, in a voice that was almost irresistible.

"I'll play for ten minutes, that's your lot," said Chrissie. "And for heaven's sake, don't pass me the ball – you'll be disappointed."

Nisha chuckled and called out to her teammates, "I've recruited another to our team." She headed back towards the makeshift pitch, Chrissie trailing behind her. "Maz, Sophie, this is Chrissie." A couple of wet muddy shapes in shorts waved at her, smiles showing through the rain.

"Remember," said Chrissie, "no passing to me!"

"Right you are," said Nisha, immediately kicking the ball towards her friend.

Chrissie squealed, the ball making a muddy imprint on her raincoat. It fell to the ground and she swung her leg. Her foot made contact and the ball flew into the sky before landing less than a metre from her.

"See," said Nisha, "you're a natural."

Chrissie grimaced, but inside she was laughing. This was fun. She couldn't remember the last time she'd done something daft, something that didn't directly 'do good' for anyone. She was doing something just because she fancied it. And it was fun.

This was new.

"Your ball," called one of the other players towards Chrissie, and she ran towards it before kicking it off the pitch and into a tree.

She laughed. "Sorry!" The good-natured players waved away her apologies and one patted her on the back.

While she didn't feel she'd really got the hang of it, there was a freedom to running up and down the pitch in the rain, shouting when the ball came near her, sharing in cheers when a goal was scored – or groaning when it just missed.

"Ok, everyone," said Sophie, the tall goalie, "that's us for the day. See you next week!"

Goodbyes were said and the women vanished quickly to their homes, their children, their partners, their hot showers.

Chrissie and Nisha were the last of the footballers left in the park, strangely unwilling to leave.

"Do you remember that night when it rained?" asked Nisha. She turned towards the park's exit and Chrissie followed.

Chrissie's voice caught in her throat. "Of course I do," she said. They were both dripping, but the rain was beginning to ease, and they carried along down the road together. "We were stuck in the back garden, even though you needed the loo."

"Oh God, yes," said Nisha. She paused, not looking across to Chrissie, who felt her pulse quicken. "It felt like we were on an island, thousands of miles away from anyone else."

Still walking, Chrissie looked at Nisha, whose eyes were

on the ground, her hair sparkling with raindrops. "I felt like that too."

Neither of them spoke, but in silent agreement they had ended up on Chrissie's doorstep.

But they weren't the only ones.

There was a man standing there with a large golfing umbrella, long white hair and a blank expression on his face.

"What the hell are you doing here?" asked Chrissie, blood roaring in her ears.

Chapter Fifteen

The night it rained was two weeks into their garden stay. The tent had become their home, and Chrissie and Nisha retreated there each night to sleep, side by side in their sleeping bags. It had been a hot and humid day, and the storm that hit was almost therapeutic in its violence. It had broken the intimate moment that had come so close to opening up between the two girls. There was the immediate scent of petrichor, and a deafening pummelling of raindrops on the canvas.

"I hope it's waterproof," said Nisha, looking up nervously.

"We're about to find out," replied Chrissie, smiling. "But a little bit of water won't harm us." She looked up. "It seems to be holding."

There was a crash of thunder. "Wow," said Nisha. "I'm not going to be able to have a wee any time soon, am I? I should have gone earlier when we got the ice-cream."

"Not if you want to stay dry," said Chrissie, buzzing

with the storm and the feelings swirling inside her. "Come on, let me distract you."

Nisha raised her eyebrows. Chrissie continued: "This book is really good. I can sense something is about to happen. I'll read it to you."

"Alright," said Nisha, lying back, her hands behind her head. Chrissie sat cross legged beside her, enjoying their closeness.

Chrissie began to read. *"Lady Amelia needed to get to the stables, to find Pine, the stable hand. She couldn't wait any longer for answers. What on earth was Pine thinking, coming into the manor house, leaving her a note? She had no interest in a secret tryst with someone whose job was to care for the horses. How dare Pine assume that she would."*

"Ooh, secret tryst," said Nisha, "I'm interested now."

"Shh," said Chrissie, before continuing. *"She arrived to find Pine perched on a hay bale, sipping from a hip flask. 'My father will hear of this, Pine,' she spat. 'I have no idea why you thought you could send me such a note and believe you would keep your position here.' Pine stood and walked towards Amelia, smirking before speaking: 'I think you know full well why I sent you that note, m'Lady. After the riding session yesterday, I think you made it very clear what you wanted.' Colour rose in Amelia's cheeks, but she couldn't place exactly why. 'Pine,' she started, but was cut off by the stable hand. 'Really, m'Lady, I think you should use my first name. Sarah.' Amelia felt something that was like fury, but not fury, build in her chest."*

"Sarah?" exclaimed Nisha. Chrissie felt her own cheeks warm, and adjusted her position so she was lying beside Nisha, rather than looking at her. She could feel heat emanating from her friend's arm, but tried to block it out somewhere between the book and the pounding rain.

Chrissie continued to read. *"'You are impudent, Sarah Pine,' said Amelia, although her voice had now softened. 'What if I am?'*

replied Sarah, with a wink. 'I think you've had enough of people bowing and scraping.' Sarah took the lady's hand and bowed low and long, before kissing her knuckles. 'Sarah,' said Amelia, barely above a whisper. The stable hand straightened. 'Amelia,' she said, no more teasing in her eyes, only desire."

"Only desire!" scoffed Nisha.

"Shush," said Chrissie, annoyed that Nisha seemed to be making light of the story. "Amelia stepped forward, grabbed Sarah's ragged collar and pressed their lips together. A moan came from Amelia, as Sarah pushed her back towards a gnarled oak post in the stable wall." Chrissie stopped reading. She didn't know if she should continue. She didn't want to risk Nisha's ridicule. But she wanted to know what happened next, and what surprised her most was that she wanted Nisha to know as well.

"Why did you stop?" asked Nisha, pushing herself up on one elbow.

"You think it's silly," said Chrissie, an edge to her voice that she didn't recognise.

"When did you become a mind reader? You don't know what I'm thinking right now."

The rain beat a rhythm on the canvas, hiding the way Chrissie's breath quickened. "I can guess," she said, raising her voice over the sound of the torrent.

"You're guessing wrong," Nisha told her, turning on her side to face her friend. "But what I want to know is what you're thinking? Why are you so sensitive about this?"

Chrissie remained resolutely on her back. She felt like Nisha was teasing her, that she had been found out, some-how. That Nisha could see that the story had made Chrissie blush, that it had given words to something she had been feeling. Something she had been feeling about Nisha. She was irrationally angry with Nisha about this, even though she knew this was unfair.

"Talk to me, Chris," said Nisha, laying a cool hand on Chrissie's forearm. Chrissie could feel goosebumps forming immediately beneath it, and was tempted to pull it away. But she didn't. She lay there, still, breathing. Nisha stayed silent, knowing her tent-mate well enough to realise sometimes it was better to wait for her to organise her thoughts.

Chrissie sighed. "Alright," she said. "Ok, I like this book. I like this story. It's so much more exciting than anything else I've read." The words seemed to release her, and she turned on her side to face Nisha. "It's more exciting than any boy I've kissed. It means more, it feels more and I'm not sure what that means."

"I think you know what that means," said Nisha. Chrissie could feel her friend's breath on her face. "And you're not alone."

Chrissie closed her eyes, overwhelmed by the sounds, the feelings, the sensations pulsing through her.

"Chris, look at me," said Nisha. "Don't you think there's a reason I come and sleep in a musty old tent with you every night?"

Chrissie's eyes, now open, widened. "Because?" she whispered.

Nisha paused for a moment before moving closer to Chrissie, and gently parted her lips before laying them softly on her friend's.

Chrissie felt how soft Nisha was, how well their mouths fitted together, how normal this felt, while her heart beat a rhythm it had never created before. A low, powerful spark made its way from her mouth down to her stomach, and she leaned into the kiss.

Nisha pulled away slowly, looking at Chrissie, and then

easing back so they were lying side by side again. Chrissie pulled Nisha's fingers into her own, and they lay like that, staring at the canvas and its fairy-light adornments in silence. The rain was slowing, revealing the sound of the girls' breaths.

After five or six minutes had passed, Chrissie finally spoke.

"I thought it was just me."

Chapter Sixteen

C hrissie could feel Nisha's eyes staring into her face, searching for a clue as to who this man standing before them was.

He shrugged, and gave a charming smile. His curly hair was long and unkempt, and he was wearing open-toed sandals. His toes, impossibly tanned. "You know why I'm here, Christina," he said.

Chrissie felt a shiver down her back. It wasn't the rain that had somehow made it through her raincoat chilling her. It was the person before her. She had hoped never to see him again.

She took a deep breath and set her face. "I want you to go, Lucian," she said in a quiet but firm voice.

"I just want to talk," replied Lucian, the man who had led Chrissie and the others into such confusion and misery just a few short years before.

"I don't want to talk with you," said Chrissie. "Now please step aside and leave me alone." She could feel her voice wobbling. She could feel her hand tremble as she raised her key.

"You know we never finished our work," said Lucian, his charming smile now replaced with a hardness. "I can't protect you from yourself if you don't come back."

There was an invisible pull to him that Chrissie hated, but had to acknowledge was there. He had dominated her life, controlled her every thought and deed for almost three years.

"You heard her," said Nisha. Chrissie looked across in surprise. She'd forgotten Nisha was there. "She asked you to leave."

The man ignored Nisha, concentrating his laser gaze on Chrissie. "I can see that you have come a long way from the path. And many in my position would let you go. But I can see so much potential in you," he added. "And I'm not ready to give up."

Nisha squared up to the man, in spite of him being almost a foot taller than her. She spoke very quietly, but very clearly and with menace. "You leave now, like she told you, or I will call the police right now." She lifted her right hand, showing her phone. Chrissie could feel the adrenalin pumping through her body, her limbs getting ready to run.

But Nisha wasn't moving. She glared at Lucian in a manner that scared Chrissie. She was afraid of what he would do.

He looked down at Nisha. "I see," he said. He looked over Nisha's head at Chrissie. "You know how to find me." Nisha didn't move, forcing him to walk around her. But then, to Chrissie's relief, he walked away and down the street, leaving them behind.

Nisha took the keys from Chrissie and opened the door. They went up the stairs to Chrissie's flat. Energy and anger and relief and something else pulsed through Chrissie, and as the front door of her flat closed behind her she grasped Nisha's shoulders, pushed her against the wall, and kissed her. It was artless and rough, but she felt thirsty for Nisha's mouth. And Nisha, seemingly stunned at first, kissed her right back, pulling Chrissie in closer.

There was a familiarity to the feel of Nisha's lips on hers, her hands on her waist. But there was something new, as well. It had been a long time since they had kissed, and there was something more urgent in this moment, as their soaking faces pressed together.

Their sodden clothes clung together and reality began to seep in. "Oh God," said Chrissie, breaking away. "I'm sorry. I didn't even ask permission."

Nisha chuckled. "No, bab, you didn't. But you may recall that I kissed you back." Her dimple was on full show and her damp cheeks were pink. She looked at Chrissie with a desire Chrissie didn't know what to do with.

"I'm sorry, I wasn't thinking. It was all too much and then you were there, and you made him leave. I was overwhelmed." Chrissie stood back, looking down at the damp patch on the carpet onto which they had both dripped.

"Stop apologising, please," said Nisha. "Really, it's fine." A beat. "Are you ok?"

"I'm all over the place," said Chrissie, shivering, although whether it was through lust, cold or fear, she couldn't tell.

"Can I suggest that before we do anything else, you have a hot shower?" said Nisha, motioning to them both. "I think you need warming up." Her eyes sparkled, and she looked as though she was about to say something else, but then decided against it.

"Yes, you're probably right. I think you need one, too," Chrissie replied.

"Well, you go first," said Nisha, gently placing a hand on the arm of Chrissie's muddy raincoat. Chrissie wondered briefly whether her fingers might leave some kind of imprint.

Chapter Seventeen

Chrissie emerged from the shower into her bedroom feeling much more human. She wasn't sure what had just happened, or why, but she was glad she hadn't been alone when Lucian appeared. She had thought – hoped – that she would never see him again. She didn't understand how he could still continue to peddle his lies and manipulations anymore. But there he'd been, in broad daylight, on the doorstep of her home. She shuddered. Her judgement had been so bad when it came to him and his followers. She silently berated herself in just the way her therapist had advised her not to, and then pulled the thought back, reminding herself she should show the same kindness to herself that she liked to show to others. Easier said than done. What scared her was the pull towards Lucian she had felt. All this time, all the work she had done. Her rules. But still, he had a hold over her that terrified her.

Once she had pulled on some jogging bottoms and a hoody, she went into the kitchen, where she did a double take. Nisha had stripped down to some boy shorts and a vest top, underneath which her sports bra could be clearly seen through the rain-soaked material. For a moment, Nisha didn't notice her. She was pouring out two steaming cups of tea with her back to Chrissie. Chrissie could feel her cheeks flush and her fingers tingle, but it was nothing to do with the shower.

"Um," said Chrissie, unable to form any words that made sense.

"I assumed you wanted something hot," said Nisha, passing a mug over to Chrissie, whose brain was now fizzing.

"Mhm," said Chrissie, taking the comment at face value, making a supreme effort not to read anything further into it, and to keep her eyes on her tea-maker's face.

"You still drink herbals, right?"

Safer territory for Chrissie. "Yes," she said.

Nisha paused and looked into Chrissie's face, her eyes soft. "You ok?"

"It's all been a lot today," said Chrissie, pleased she was able to form a sentence, but still unable to stop her skin from tingling. Even her knees felt weird. Was she having some kind of medical crisis?

Nisha frowned. "That man?" she asked.

Chrissie nodded, although there was a lot more going on for her than that. "The shower's free," she said, not sure what else to do or say.

Nisha winked. "So I see," she replied. She vanished out of the kitchen.

Chrissie leaned against the kitchen surface and gave a long sigh. "Wowsers," she said out loud. "I did that," she added, before running her own tongue along her top lip, the memory of Nisha's mouth on hers.

"You did what?" came Nisha's voice, her head poking round the door.

Chrissie abruptly stood up straight. "Ah, um, played football."

"That you did," said Nisha. "Does it matter what towel I use?"

"Oh, yeah, use one of the clean ones on the top shelf by the sink," Chrissie told her. Nisha gave her a thumbs up before disappearing back into the bathroom.

Today had not been a good day for her adrenaline levels. Or her emotions, for that matter. She desperately needed Nisha to go. But she also desperately wanted to kiss her again. To do more than kiss her. To undress her, to be close to her, to touch her.

But somewhere inside, Chrissie knew she needed to pay attention to two of her rules. Firstly, she had to examine this, question it, find out what it was about, why it was happening. What was Nisha's agenda? What did she want? Why did she want it? What did Chrissie want? And why?

And of course, at the heart of it all, she knew that she couldn't allow herself to fall in love.

But a kiss wasn't love, right?

It wasn't not love though, either.

And it had happened immediately after seeing Lucian again for the first time in over a year. The man that had controlled her, had scared her, and had changed her. She couldn't let a reaction to seeing him shape the rest of her life – or even the rest of the week. That would be a dangerous path.

She needed her journal, she needed her pens. She really needed time to herself, in spite of her body betraying her, desperate for another kiss, desperate to feel Nisha's hands on her again.

Chrissie's mind drifted to the woman she could hear in the shower, and she found it hard not to imagine the rivulets of water flowing down her skin, the steam enveloping her shape, the soap sliding across her features. She screwed up her eyes and shook her head.

No. She couldn't do this.

Chapter Eighteen

"You seemed a bit distracted today," said Rae, as they and Chrissie packed away the yoga mats.

"Mmm," replied Chrissie. "It's been a pretty intense few days. For a start, Lucian showed up on my doorstep."

"Oh my God," said Rae, momentarily pausing their clearing up. "Are you ok? Do you need to talk?"

Chrissie nodded. Her mind had been a blur of circular thinking and rumination for the remainder of the weekend after she'd kissed Nisha.

"Come on then," said Rae. "Let's go for a stroll down by the River Rea. It's not far from here, and I hear there've been a few kingfisher sightings."

"Sounds ideal," agreed Chrissie, relieved to have someone to share her thoughts with. She needed to sort herself out before work on Monday.

They made their way down Vicarage Road, towards the bottom of Cartland Road, where they picked up the river. Abruptly, they went from urban sprawl to a green haven for wildlife, soothed by the babble of flowing water.

As they walked, Chrissie told her friend about the previous day, leaving nothing out, aside from the daydreaming about Nisha in the shower. That didn't need to be shared with anyone else, although she couldn't deny that she'd replayed the thought a few times in solitude since the previous afternoon.

"How did you leave it?" asked Rae, once the whole tale had been told. One of the things Chrissie valued about them as a friend was that they were such a good listener, and made the time to hear everything, not asking questions or jumping in with advice.

"It was all a bit awkward," said Chrissie, biting her lip. "I said I was feeling overwhelmed by seeing Lucian and that I needed to be on my own. I think she wanted to talk."

"Talk?" said Rae with a friendly grin.

"Well," replied Chrissie, "I got the sense she felt we had unfinished business. Which of course is true, and not just from yesterday."

"You'll have to tell me more about that another time," said Rae. "But did you leave things ok?"

"I think so," said Chrissie. "She accepted I needed a bit of time. She was very sweet, actually. She gave me a hug and told me to call her if I needed her." She didn't tell Rae that she'd held onto the hug for a little longer than was strictly necessary and almost reversed her own decision that nothing further should happen in that moment. Nisha had followed up with a text message an hour later, checking in on Chrissie. Her kindness was genuinely touching, and it went straight into her journal, along with everything else that had happened.

And the never-ending questions.

"Do you think, perhaps, that there might be something here to be explored?" asked Rae, a note of caution in their voice. Chrissie had told them how hesitant she was to be involved – with anyone – many times.

"It's too complicated. We have all this history," said Chrissie, letting her hand brush against the leaves drooping from the trees on the banks of the river, still glistening with raindrops. "And I just don't think I'm ready to be with anyone. I don't think I can be trusted not to ruin everything."

"Do you not think we all feel a bit like that?" asked Rae.

"Do you?"

"Well, yes, actually. I do, sometimes," said Rae. They ruffled their hair and gave a rueful smile.

"And there's me, obsessing about myself and going on about all that's happening in my life. I haven't even asked about you," said Chrissie, berating herself for having now managed to ignore all three of her rules this weekend, to a greater or lesser extent.

"It's no biggie," said Rae. "I've just started seeing someone. No drama. But I definitely get what you mean about being afraid to wreck everything. She's so lovely and fun and sparky. I don't want to spoil it."

"Right, we're officially pausing my debacle of a life for the moment, tell me about her, I'm desperate to know!"

Rae smiled, their cheeks going pink. "She's called Clodagh. She's gorgeous and funny and very sexy. She's a physio at the hospital. Very clever, great company."

"She sounds perfect for you," said Chrissie. "You're such a wonderful friend, I can only imagine you'd make a brilliant partner."

"Aw, that's a lovely thing to say," said Rae. "And the thing is," they continued, "the same can be said of you."

"We're not conflating those two things," Chrissie told them, gently. "I know that maybe one day I might be in a position to give someone a proper loving relationship, but I have work to do on myself." She kicked a stone into the undergrowth. "I'm not the finished article."

"Are any of us?" said Rae.

"Look!" whispered Chrissie urgently. She pointed to a flash of royal blue and dark orange.

"The kingfisher!" said Rae. They both stopped, their breaths almost held so as not to startle the creature that was so rarely seen here.

The bird hovered and flitted around the tree roots and dangling shrubs that met the flowing river. It popped in and out of the foliage, occasionally disappearing and then emerging somewhere else.

A figure in purple lycra was heading in their direction. Chrissie turned slightly and gestured quietly to the jogger to pause. "The kingfisher!" she whispered, hoping the runner would understand. The figure slowed, and then smiled.

"Hello," she said in a voice just above a whisper, recognition in her face.

"Hello!" exclaimed Chrissie, her heart sinking slightly. It was Dottie's mum, the ever-present over-involved parent.

"Wow," said the woman, catching sight of the regal bird. "What a wonderful sight." She pressed pause on her running watch, and wiped sweat from her brow.

"Yeah," agreed Rae, a wide smile on their face.

After a few moments, the kingfisher flew off away into the greenery of the woods around the river. The three figures sighed in unison and there was a brief, enjoyable silence.

"Do you have ten minutes for me tomorrow after school?" asked Dottie's mum. Chrissie set her expression, trying not to hide her surprise at being accosted like this on a Sunday walk. "I'd ask you now, but I need to finish my run

– I'm on a strict training plan for the 10k next week," she said.

"Sure," said Chrissie. "In fact, you might be able to help me with something."

"Perfect," said Philippa, pressing the button on her watch and trotting off along the River Rea.

Chapter Nineteen

It was another awkward morning, and Chrissie couldn't work out if the butterflies in her stomach were down to looking forward to seeing Nisha, or dreading it.

She turned the corner on her walk to work and saw the school gates. Her heart beat faster, and she almost tripped over her own feet. She stopped and shook her head. This was why this was such a bad idea. She needed to put an end to it. Whatever it was. And in truth, it had just been a moment of madness.

Hadn't it?

A child whizzed past her on a scooter, bringing her out of her thoughts. A harried-looking father jogged to keep up. "Come on, love," he said, "we need to get to Asda to get some stuff for tea, don't go too far ahead." He met Chrissie's eyes briefly and smiled. She smiled back, recognising him from the playground, and wondering if there was someone waiting for him and his daughter later today. Did he have a teammate, or was he parenting alone? She knew plenty of children who only had one parent, or travelled between two who lived separately. Kings Heath had a diverse community with a wide variety of family units. Chrissie was always particularly impressed with those who had complex blended families, with step-parents and siblings, but somehow managed to navigate the peaks and troughs of family life so well.

Chrissie's phone beeped, pulling her from her reverie. Nisha's name flashed up. Her stomach flipped. What couldn't wait for her to arrive in the classroom in the next few minutes?

Nisha's message read: "Really bad timing, but I've come down with some kind of nasty flu bug thing. Can't come in today, and probably not for a couple of days. Ernest (Hemingway) says she has a plan."

Chrissie giggled at the new nickname for Mrs Hemingway, and was caught between relief that she didn't have to have a conversation with Nisha today, and worry that Nisha was sick. But there was little time to think that through. She arrived in her classroom to find Dan there already.

"Good morning," he said, "it's going to be a busy couple of days. Nisha's poorly, so I'm covering her class as well as mine."

Chrissie nodded. Dan's class was next door to hers, so it made sense. It would mean more work for her, but she didn't feel too phased by the prospect. She'd got to know the children pretty well by now, and they were a nice class.

"Just let me know what you need me to do," she said.

"Well, if you can sort out the numeracy this morning, we can regroup at lunchtime, perhaps?"

"Sure, I'm on it," she said, feeling a strange pride in being trusted to lead the class herself for the first time.

"I'll pop my head in now and again, and obviously give

me a shout if one of the kids goes feral," said Dan with a wink.

Chrissie laughed. "Noted."

The children were, typically, scandalised by the absence of Ms Rajan, immediately conjuring up various conspiracy theories about what had happened to her. Chrissie calmly went through what they needed to work on that morning, trying to ignore Dottie's insistence that Ms Rajan had been kidnapped by aliens.

"I know, because I saw a weird green light outside my bedroom window last night," said the girl, her eyes wide. Two other children gasped.

"If I could ask you to please get your numeracy books out and sit down as quickly as possible, that would be grand," said Chrissie. "And for the record, Ms Rajan has not been kidnapped by aliens." All the children looked up at her. "She is carrying out fieldwork with them, and will be back on Earth very soon."

The children's faces were a cross between surprise and hilarity. Dottie just nodded sagely. "Told you," she said to her friends.

"Francis," said Chrissie, "are you ok?"

"I can't find my book," said the small boy, who had been slowly gaining in confidence in the few weeks since he joined the school. But this morning his eyes filled with tears.

Chrissie crouched down so she was on the same level as him. "I'll help you." She paused, then whispered. "It's ok, Ms Rajan isn't really on a spaceship. She'll be back in a couple of days."

Francis gave a small smile. "Good. I miss her," he said.

It wasn't long before the class was settled to their task. Chrissie took a moment to surreptitiously message Nisha: "I'm so sorry you're poorly. Are you ok? Do you need anything? We're fine here. Me and Dan are keeping the show on the road. x"

The dots on the screen told her Nisha had started replying straight away, a sure sign that she was bored. A moment later, the message appeared: "Thanks, bab. I'm fine. Just sorry to land this on you. Hope the kids are ok. I know we need to talk, right? When I'm better x"

Chrissie couldn't answer straight away, due to an impending number stick emergency. By the time she got back to her phone it was lunchtime. There was another message from Nisha: "Really hope I haven't given this to you ;) x"

Chrissie shivered slightly. It was the first time either of them had properly acknowledged the kiss, and her body's response was very different to her brain's.

Chapter Twenty

M anaging the class by herself had been tiring, but Chrissie had enjoyed it. At home that evening, she opened her journal and began to write:

"Maybe this is something I can do. Maybe I could teach. It would be an incredible way to give back to so many people. It could really start to make up for the mistakes I have made. A chance for atonement, perhaps."

She picked up a turquoise pen and drew a cloud around her words, before adding more below:

"But I cannot be pushed off course by selfish desires. The kiss between me and Nisha was a momentary thing, a memory of twenty years ago. I need to remember my rules: Give back, of course, but the others, too. Don't fall in love. Question everything. I cannot go backwards, only forwards. And I need to know who I really am before I let anyone else into my life."

Chrissie felt a calm descend as she closed the book. Yes, she would be fine. Nisha would understand.

She picked up her phone and messaged Rebecca, the

vicar, enthused by her day with her class. An hour later Chrissie found herself in the church – not a space she normally entered by choice.

"I won't bite," came Rebecca's voice, echoing through the empty gothic space.

Chrissie smiled, uneasily. Questioning everything was hard, and she wasn't sure whether being in a place of worship suited her. By its very nature, faith did not come with evidence. And Chrissie had put her faith in the wrong people before, with devastating consequences. What she needed now was evidence.

Rebecca gave a wave from the front of the church where she was arranging flowers by the altar.

Chrissie walked towards her friend, taking in the coolness and calmness of the place. She might not have been religious herself, but she could appreciate the solace that some people found in the building.

"I'm leading a funeral tomorrow," said Rebecca, brightly. "So I want to make sure there are plenty of flowers around the place."

"Sounds perfect. Where do I start?" asked Chrissie, pleased to have a practical task to complete. Flowers for a funeral were less an article of faith, more a symbol of comfort, and that was something she could get on board with.

The pair chatted as they worked, the vicar's round figure clad in a hoodie today, rather than the dog collar she would wear the following day.

"So," said Rebecca, a while into their conversation, "you need to conjure up some cash for this trip to Paris, right? And we need to work out how to do it."

"Exactly. Not all the kids' families would be able to afford it, and I really don't think that we should be doing it unless they can all go," replied Chrissie, gathering some yellow blooms together to go into one of the vases.

"Well, I fully support that," said Rebecca, "but you have set yourself something of a steep task. That said, it's probably easier raising funds for kids to go to France than it is for feeding those that some would rather pretend don't exist, like we do here." She screwed up her face to indicate she was thinking hard. Chrissie knew Rebecca would be able to help. She was endlessly creative and well used to strong-arming people into providing time and money in aid of those less fortunate.

"Thanks, Rebecca. I realise this isn't feeding the needy, but I do think it's worth doing," said Chrissie, moving onto the next arrangement of flowers.

"It's all legitimate, my dear." Rebecca was working at twice the speed of Chrissie, who was no slouch herself. The vicar's efficiency was the stuff of legend. "Everyone deserves a chance to see something amazing. For these kids, maybe it's the Eiffel Tower." She finished the vase she was working on. "Et voila! We're done. Thank you so much for your help."

"You're welcome," said Chrissie, happy that her handi-work might make what would be a difficult day a little easier.

"I'll have a bit of a think about your trip funds, but in the meantime, how well do you know these kids' parents? Kings Heath has a bit of everything, and I wouldn't be surprised if there are one or two mums or dads who are well connected with some of the big companies in the city centre. They like to do their bit for 'the community'," she put air quotes around the words. "Be careful with the conversation, mind, no one wants to feel they're being pumped for cash, but most people like the idea of being able to help," she added, as the pair of them walked towards the big wooden front door of the church. The vicar was already pulling out her cigarettes in preparation for an impending smoking break.

"That's a really good point," said Chrissie, making a mental note to ask Dan what he knew. He'd taught her class when they were back in Year One. He might have some suggestions.

Chrissie strolled back towards her home, a spring in her step. Rebecca always made her feel like anything was possible. She would start afresh tomorrow and make this happen. She wanted to share her newfound positivity, and pulled out her phone to message Nisha. Then she paused. Should she contact her again today, given what she'd already decided?

Yes, she decided. They were colleagues and friends. This would be fine.

"How are you feeling now, poorly person?" she wrote. "I've done a flower-arranging shift in return for some fundraising advice from the vicar x"

Chapter Twenty-One

"Oh, good morning, Miss Anderson. So sorry I missed you earlier this week," said Dottie's mum. Chrissie was letting the children in and tried not to let a pained expression reveal her sinking heart at hearing the woman's voice.

"Good morning, how are you?" replied Chrissie, using the professional voice she'd developed for just these conversations, where she needed to be friendly, but not overly encouraging of long conversation. Nisha still wasn't back, so she couldn't hang around at the door for long.

"Good thanks, but you don't need to know about that," said Philippa. "I just wanted to say that I've heard about your proposal to take the class to Paris."

"Um, you have?" said Chrissie, surprised. They hadn't mentioned it to the children, because they didn't know if they'd be able to pull it off yet.

"Yes, Dottie told me she heard you talking about it," replied her mother. Chrissie was feeling the similarity between the two busy-bodies. "And anyway, I wanted to say that if you need any help, or support, please do let me know."

"Right," said Chrissie. "Well, thank you. Actually, we were wondering if you might be willing to talk about helping us out with the trip itself," she continued, remembering the conversation with Dan. "Perhaps we could have a conversation about it at a different time?"

"Absolutely, please do," said Philippa. "I won't keep you, I know you have the children to deal with. But in the meantime, take my card."

"Thanks, Philippa," said Chrissie, dropping the card into the pocket of her skirt. It was one of her favourites, precisely because it was a rare one that actually had pockets. Philippa gave a wave and darted off. Chrissie walked to the front of the class, hoping she was doing the right thing by involving Dottie's mum.

"Excuse me, class, this is supposed to be a school, not a Taylor Swift concert. Can you all please take of your coats, hang them up and sit down at your tables?" she said.

"What's your favourite Taylor Swift song, Miss," came a small voice. Chrissie looked down. It was, of course, Dottie, who had taken off her coat in double quick time. Like mother, like daughter.

"It's a toss-up between *Blank Space* and *High Infidelity*, I think," said Chrissie, having learnt more about the American singer in the last year than she ever thought possible, thanks to the children she supported.

"Good choice," said Dottie. "Mine is any song off TTPD."

"Excellent," replied Chrissie. "Now, please go and sit down." Dottie sloped off to join the other children.

It wasn't until later in the day that she looked at the card Philippa had given her.

Philippa Samfire
Founding Partner
Chase, Wilson and Samfire LLP

Founding partner of one of the city's biggest law firms? Chrissie had known the woman worked in a law firm, but she hadn't realised she was a founding partner. An idea began to form in Chrissie's head and immediately she texted Nisha: "How are you? Well enough for visitors? I have news. x"

Nisha responded immediately, indicating she was bored beyond words and needed company. Chrissie's heart gave a leap, before she reminded herself that this was strictly work, and perhaps a little bit of looking out for her friend.

"I'll bring your tea over after school x" texted Chrissie.

Chrissie swung by the local supermarket on her way to Nisha's place. She'd not been in Nisha's space before, and was curious to see what it was like. She grabbed some fresh bread rolls and a carton of organic chicken soup. That was what poorly people needed, right?

She arrived at a modern-looking apartment block that had sprung up a few years before not far from Kings Heath High Street, and pressed the button for Nisha.

"Come on up," came a distant voice through the crackly intercom system.

Chrissie made her way up to the second floor to find the door to Nisha's flat was already open for her. Nisha was in the doorway, looking slightly pale, but smiling, wearing grey joggers and a blue hoodie.

"Hey," said Nisha.

Chrissie felt suddenly shy. She hadn't seen Nisha since 'the kiss', and her own body felt suddenly alien to her, as if she needed to think through every move very carefully.

"Hey, how are you? Are you feeling any better?" she asked, trying to walk in and take off her coat like a normal person. She wasn't sure if she'd succeeded.

"Oh, I'm getting there. I reckon I'll be back at school by the end of the week. Sorry in advance for the mess, though," said Nisha, a sheepish smile on her face.

The modern apartment was strewn with blankets and cushions and empty glasses, cereal bowls and boxes of tissues. "Oh, it could be so much worse," said Chrissie, feeling for her friend.

"Um, can I possibly have a hug?" asked Nisha, in an uncharacteristically timid voice. "I know I'm a strong independent woman and all that, but it's at times like this that I miss having someone there."

Chrissie's heart warmed before melting. "Of course," she said, opening her arms and beckoning Nisha in

"I'm such a wimp," came a muffled voice from Chrissie's shoulder.

"No you're not," Chrissie told her, breathing in the freshly laundered scent of Nisha's loungewear. There was something comforting about their bodies being close together, something that made Chrissie feel more whole, somehow. She had felt hollow for so long. Lost in her own thoughts, the embrace lasted far longer than she had planned.

"Thanks, Chris," said Nisha, rubbing her hands up Chrissie's back.

"No problem," said Chrissie, her head and body a whirl of emotions. She could just kiss Nisha now. It would feel so right to almost every part of her. But her brain screamed no. They moved apart, and Chrissie stepped away awkwardly. "Let me have a little tidy-up for you, and then I'll make you some soup."

"You're the best," said Nisha, collapsing back onto her sofa, seemingly unaffected by the embrace. Chrissie couldn't help but remember how everything had ended twenty years earlier. She didn't want to go there again.

Chrissie shrugged off her wistful thoughts and got to work, whipping the living room into shape before making soup for them both.

"Thanks," said Nisha, settling back on the sofa with a mug of chicken soup. "I know I've already said it, but you really are the best. I really appreciate you coming over and feeding me." Chrissie smiled, but didn't say anything. There was too much to say, and none of it made any sense right now.

Chapter Twenty-Two

"So, you're saying that this Philippa woman might actually hold the solution to all our problems?" asked Nisha, colour returning to her cheeks now she'd finished her soup.

"Well, perhaps not all," said Chrissie, "but it certainly sounds like she's someone worth having a chat with." She sighed. "She's a bit extra, always wanting to tell me every detail of her daughter's needs each morning before school. I do find her quite tiring."

"Well we're in no position to be fussy," said Nisha. "I reckon we make a plan to meet up with her and find out what she can offer us, beyond just coming along on the trip. Law firms have loads of cash, right?"

"Well, more than schools do, yes. I think you're right," agreed Chrissie.

"Always," said Nisha, with a grin. "God, that soup hit the spot. I'm feeling much better."

"I'm really pleased," said Chrissie. "It's not been the same without you at school. I mean, me and Dan have coped, but, you know…" She trailed off, unsure what to say next.

"Do you think we ought to talk?" asked Nisha.

"Um, we are talking," said Chrissie, not wanting to look directly at Nisha, who was sitting next to her.

"Don't be obtuse," said Nisha. "You know what I mean." Chrissie pressed her lips together. Nisha continued. "You kissed me."

Chrissie's eyes closed and she breathed in. "Yes, I know. I'm sorry. I shouldn't have done that. It was a weird moment in a weird day," she said, her words tumbling out one after another. "I didn't ask your consent and it wasn't ok and I really don't know what came over me." She was about to say more, but Nisha held up her hand.

"Hang on a minute, Chris, you kissed me, yes. And I'm not going to lie, I was surprised. But I kissed you back," said Nisha, her face turning slightly towards the woman by her side. "I was involved, too."

Chrissie felt a mixture of relief and excitement, but then confusion. She needed to get all her words out now, before Nisha said anything more. "Ok, yes, you were there too," she agreed. "But it wasn't the right thing. I'm in a really vulnerable place right now. I don't know who I can trust, and I'm still only rebuilding my life."

Nisha stayed quiet this time, and let Chrissie talk.

"I have made terrible mistakes and I have hurt people, people who didn't deserve it. I shouldn't have kissed you. It was wrong of me. It was about what happened back after our exams that summer, not about now."

"So you're saying it was a mistake?" said Nisha, her brow furrowed.

"I'm saying I can't trust my instincts, and I'm not in a place to be in a relationship."

"Ah yes, the rules," said Nisha, giving a grimace.

"I know you think they're stupid, but after everything that happened, I have to have some framework to live by," Chrissie replied. She placed her hands on her knees, smoothing her trousers.

"I don't think they're stupid," said Nisha in a soft voice, "and I am really sorry I got so cross that day at the Vine. I shouldn't have. But I'll be real with you, I don't understand them. I sort of wonder if you're swapping one set of rules – those set by that awful cult bloke – for another, even if they are self-imposed."

"Nisha," started Chrissie, but a hand gently rested on hers.

"No, I know, this isn't my business. I get it," said Nisha. "But aside from that, tell me how you feel."

"What do you mean?" asked Chrissie, enjoying the feel of Nisha's fingers against her own.

"I mean, forgetting rules and 'shoulds' and 'shouldn'ts', do you really think that kiss was just a remnant of the past?"

"Don't you?" asked Chrissie, turning to look at Nisha properly now. Nisha squeezed Chrissie's hand.

"Honestly, I don't know. That was all such a long time ago. We were young and it was new and exciting. We're so much older now. Perhaps, even wiser."

Chrissie chuckled. "I'm not sure I am anyone's idea of a paragon of wisdom." She took a long breath out before asking the next question. The one she'd been waiting twenty years to ask. "But I still don't really know what happened, Nisha. Please, could you tell me what happened?" She looked directly into her old friend's eyes, hoping to see some explanation there.

Silence. Nisha shrugged, removed her hand and looked away. "I was a kid. I was stupid. It happens."

"It happens?" questioned Chrissie, feeling annoyance grow inside her for the first time.

"You don't have the monopoly on mistakes," said Nisha, who was fiddling with the TV remote control.

"But don't I get any form of explanation?" said Chrissie. "After all these years?"

"Who says there's an explanation to give?" Nisha shot back. Was it Chrissie's imagination or was she giving off the air of a grumpy teenager?

Chrissie thought back to what had followed the night of the rain storm.

Neither of them spoke about the kiss, or the way they felt. The next day was a quiet one, but there was a glow, a sense of comfort around them both. They moved together with ease, soaking up the sunshine, reading their respective books.

But as night came there was a crackle between them; an unspoken tension. They moved wordlessly into the tent as darkness fell, and drew together, side by side under the thin blankets. They kissed for hours, hands straying, clothing slowly abandoned. Whispers and moans and giggles escaped their mouths as they explored this new dimension to their relationship.

"I didn't know I could feel this way," said Chrissie, breathless, her head on Nisha's chest.

"Me neither," said Nisha in a whisper, her hands stroking Chrissie's dark blonde hair.

"I love you," said Chrissie, speaking the words as she thought them. She felt Nisha's heart rate quicken beneath her ear.

"I love you too," came Nisha's voice.

"We should always be this way," said Chrissie, as she fell asleep.

Back in Nisha's living room, Chrissie felt her eyes fill with tears, which irritated her even further. This was what she'd been trying to avoid. "But that night, after everything that happened that night," she said, sniffing back a sob, "you left. You waited until I was asleep, and you just left."

Nisha brought a hand to her face and rubbed her eyes. "It's what I do," she said. "I run."

Chapter Twenty-Three

The Vine was busy, but once her eyes had adjusted to the semi-darkness, Chrissie spotted Philippa across the room. She'd snagged a table by the window, and the moment she saw Chrissie she popped up and waved.

Chrissie mouthed "Hi" and walked over.

It was the lunch break at school. She'd been relieved that playground duty prevented Nisha from joining her for this conversation. Since the day of the soup, things had once again turned frosty between the pair.

"I'm so pleased you got in touch," said Philippa once they were settled with drinks. Philippa had a double espresso, while Chrissie had a chai latte. "So, what do you need. Time? Money?" She wasn't messing around.

"Well, um, all of the above, really," said Chrissie, slightly taken aback by how forward Philippa was. The woman was dressed in an expensive navy blue skirt suit with heels. The kind of outfit Chrissie would never wear.

"Marvellous. Well, I can sort out the cash, I think. We –

I mean the partners – have a community education fund we use every year in the city to support youngsters in Birmingham. We haven't done anything in Kings Heath in a few years, and funding a once-in-a-lifetime educational trip like this would fit the bill."

"I see," said Chrissie. It seemed she barely needed to do any of the talking in this meeting. "So what do you need from us?"

"Well," said Philippa, "how about you and Ms Rajan get some ballpark costs together and send them over? I'll present them to the partners and we'll go from there. How does the end of tomorrow sound to you?"

Chrissie raised her eyebrows. Philippa knew what she wanted, and she knew how to get it. "Er yes, of course."

"Now, of course, I cannot allow the company to pay for Dottie's place. That would be a conflict of interest. So I will pay personally for her," added Philippa.

"That makes sense," said Chrissie. She was beginning to see why Dottie was the way she was, and to her surprise, she was starting to warm to the woman. Perhaps there was more to her than being a helicopter parent.

"And because I do family law, I've got all the appropriate clearances. I could come on the trip too, if an extra pair of hands would be of use." Philippa drained her coffee cup. "You've got my email address. Sorry to have to dash, but I have a client in half an hour, so I'd better get going. Thanks for your time."

"No," said Chrissie, "thank you!"

And with that, Philippa was gone. Chrissie half expected a puff of smoke. She slowly raised the drink she had yet to start to her lips and began to work mentally through her next steps for the school trip. She needed to talk to Nisha and Dan about it so they could provide Philippa with some costs as soon as possible.

She frowned, thinking back to their previous conversation.

"It's what I do," Nisha had said. "I run."

"What do you mean?" Chrissie had replied.

"I mean, that's what I do," Nisha told her. "I ran out on you, and I ran out on Jake and London. I'm not proud of it. But it's just part of my DNA."

"But you said you and Jake drifted apart?"

"Yeah, we did, but I couldn't face sorting out the separation and staying in London. So I left." Chrissie had noticed a defensive note in Nisha's voice.

"But you have control over your actions, right?" she'd asked.

"Yes, I guess. But I also know what I'm like. I'm not the paragon of virtue you seem to have become," said Nisha with a sniff.

"That's not fair," Chrissie told her. "And it still doesn't explain why you ran away from me."

"I don't know," Nisha had said, with a sigh. "Look, I'm not sure it's helpful to talk about this stuff. It's ancient history. You say it was a mistake to kiss me, and I feel like shit. I think you should go so I can have a nap."

Chrissie hadn't needed telling twice. It was obvious there was more to this than Nisha was letting on, but somehow they'd gone from having an honest conversation to trading barbs. She got up, put their soup bowls in the kitchen and left, closing the front door gently behind her.

In the days that followed, Nisha had been quite frosty with her, only making eye contact when she had to, and keeping chat to a minimum. Chrissie's journal was full of prose about her colleague and old friend. But was she a friend now? Chrissie wasn't sure. They seemed to flip-flop between being close and acting like strangers. She didn't understand why everything was so hard, but if it did nothing else, it reinforced her rule. Definitely don't fall in love.

Chapter Twenty-Four

The days passed by in a whirl, thanks to Philippa, who had waved through their costs, adding an extra twenty percent onto the expenses estimate her company was providing, for what she termed 'little extras'.

Nisha and Chrissie resumed a working relationship in the classroom, but as if by silent agreement, they'd stopped talking about their lives outside school altogether. Chrissie was relieved. It took her off the emotional roller coaster she'd been on since the start of term.

Chrissie worked with Nisha, Dan and increasingly Philippa on planning the trip. Permission letters were sent out and enthusiastic children drew endless pictures of baguettes and the Eiffel Tower – and in one case, an Eiffel Tower made out of baguettes.

Chrissie's journal was more full of questions than ever before. The planning made for a good distraction during the day, but each evening, her thoughts were dominated by the events of the recent weeks, and the flashbacks she still had to the sight of Nisha making tea in her underwear in her flat after the rainstorm.

A week before the trip Chrissie found herself transitioning from 'cat' to 'cow' and back again in Rae's yoga class, breathing in all the right places, and still somehow her mind was full. She seemed unable to "breathe out the complexities of life" as Rae advised the class to do.

They caught up for their post-class drink and chat, and Rae questioned Chrissie on what was going on.

"The same, really," Chrissie told her. "I try to be friendly and a good colleague, and it's fine at work, but Nisha seems to have closed down. It's like she's pulled down the shutters." Chrissie clasped her hands together. "She's not nasty or anything, but she's not really engaging with me on anything that isn't essential. I feel like I've really messed things up, but I can't work out why."

"Have you considered that she might feel rejected by you?" asked Rae, thoughtfully.

Chrissie shrugged. "I don't really think she's into me, to be honest. It's clear she's still getting over her ex-boyfriend, and she's more interested in criticising my life choices than talking about how she feels."

"Yeah, but don't they say attack is the best form of defence?" said Rae, sipping their oat milkshake. "You said she didn't understand why you've set yourself up to be single. Is that code for her being hurt that you don't want her?"

"But she didn't want me in the first place," said Chrissie, exasperated. "She left me before, she still won't explain why, and now she's shutting me out."

"Hmm," said Rae. "I wonder."

Chrissie rolled her eyes. "Anyway, enough about me and

my misery. I'm even boring myself now. How is this Clodagh you've been seeing?"

Rae's eyes brightened as they spoke. "Oh, she's really good fun. We spent last Sunday afternoon at a street food fair and tasted everything available." Rae smiled. "She really knows how to live, you know?"

"Sounds full of beans," said Chrissie, wondering privately whether anyone could describe her in terms like that these days. Was Nisha right? Had she changed? Was she too buttoned up?

More for the journal later...

"In the best way," Rae added. "Actually, she'll be heading over here in a few minutes. We're going to a gig at the Carpenter's Arms."

"Nice," said Chrissie, "so I get to meet her. Excellent." Thinking about someone else's love life was so much more straightforward.

"But back to you just for a moment," said Rae, looking serious. "While I agree Nisha was a bit out of order in what she said to you, I do think you owe it to yourself to have a proper conversation with her. I wonder if some of the rules you set yourself a year ago might be in need of review?"

Chrissie didn't get a chance to answer, because a woman with curly shoulder-length hair and a giant smile came into the bar and flung her arms around Rae.

"Rae-Rae," said the woman who Chrissie had to assume was Clodagh, "I've missed you!"

Rae blushed – the first time Chrissie had ever seen that happened – and stood to greet Clodagh with a kiss. "Hey, Clodagh," they said, "this is my friend, Chrissie."

Clodagh's mouth twisted slightly as she looked at Chrissie, and the smile faded a little. "Hi," she said, holding out her hand for Chrissie to take. "Nice to meet you."

It seemed an oddly formal way to address her, especially given how enthusiastically she'd bundled into the café bar. "You too," said Chrissie. "Right, I need to get going," she added, feeling a sudden chill in the air. "I need to get some info over to Philippa before tomorrow."

"Good luck," said Rae. "I'm sure she can be a bit tiring."

"Ah it's ok," said Chrissie. "I think perhaps I judged her a bit harshly. She's a woman who likes to get things done, and I can get on board with that."

Chapter Twenty-Five

It was quarter to five in the morning, and the coach was ready to go. Dan had arrived with croissants and coffee and tea for everyone from the petrol station on the High Street. They sat in a row of five on the front wall of the school, their legs dangling side by side – Chrissie, Dan, Nisha, Philippa and Dottie.

"I think we can definitely call this the calm before the storm," said Nisha, bundled up against the November weather in a green hoodie.

"Without a doubt," agreed Dan.

Dottie piped up. "When are the others getting here?"

"In fifteen minutes," said her mum, patting her arm. "It won't be long. Eat your pain au chocolat."

Dottie dutifully shoved half the pastry into her mouth. Chrissie covered a smile with her hands before rubbing her sleepy eyes.

"Have we made a terrible mistake?" she asked out loud.

"Twenty-five children, one coach, four adults and a trip to Paris?" said Nisha. "What could possibly go wrong?"

"Shall I give you a list?" said Dan, stifling a yawn.

"Definitely not," replied Nisha. "I'd rather live in blissful ignorance." She took a sip of her hot drink. "And you know what, Chris, for what it's worth, you made this happen through sheer optimism. It's going to be awesome."

Chrissie raised her eyebrows in surprise. It was the first time Nisha had said anything to her that wasn't directly about the Key Stage 2 Curriculum or which children needed extra help with their maths that week. "Well, I think really Philippa is the one we need to thank," she said.

"Nonsense," said Philippa, brushing off the praise. "I was just in the right place at the right time. And to get to come along and support you brilliant people is an absolute pleasure."

The five of them fell quiet, sleepy smiles on their faces as they finished their breakfast.

Within half an hour, all was chaos. There were suitcases everywhere, children carrying an assortment of bags and rucksacks and tearful parents waving their little people off.

"Dottie," said Philippa, a pained expression on her face, "for goodness sake, get back on the coach. You've already got on and off three times now."

Nisha and Chrissie exchanged a wordless glance. At least it wasn't just her teachers that Dottie drove to distraction.

"Hiya, Francis," said Dan, saving his warmest smile for the shy boy who'd just presented himself, hanging onto a yellow toy car, his father a step behind him.

"Hello, Mr Harvey," replied Francis solemnly.

"You've arrived at just the right time. There's a seat on the coach right near the front, so you can see what the driver's doing at all times, *and* you get to see through the front window," said Dan, knowing a car-obsessed child when he saw one.

Francis' face brightened, and he turned to hug his father goodbye, before getting onto the coach.

"Nice save," said Nisha. "I thought he was going to cry, poor little thing."

"I'll keep a close eye on him," said Dan. "I don't think he's been away from home overnight before."

"I don't think many of them have," Chrissie chimed in, as she slid the last of the bags into the storage area at the bottom of the coach.

"I hope we're all ready for an onslaught of homesickness, then," said Nisha.

"Yeah," agreed Dan. "Mostly from me. I'm missing darts night at the pub for this."

Nisha laughed. "And I'm missing football."

"Oh, shush, you two," said Chrissie. "You'll be eating baguettes and snails before you know it."

"Ugh," said Dan, going slightly pale.

"Don't knock it 'til you've tried it," said Philippa, appearing beside them. "They're all on. I've done a head count and I think we're complete, but one of you should probably do the same."

Nisha looked again at Chrissie. They climbed onto the coach and Nisha whispered to her. "Why do I feel like she's in charge?"

Chrissie giggled. "I think she is. Let's get counting." She was relieved that some of the ice between them had started to thaw. She wasn't sure what the future held, but these last few weeks had been really difficult. She'd even started to wonder if she ought to get a job in a different school.

But now, looking down the length of the coach, into the

excited faces of all the children she'd spent the last few weeks getting to know, she knew she couldn't leave them. She owed it to them to hang on in there, even if it was a bit tricky. It was, after all, part of her mission to give back.

Chapter Twenty-Six

The scenery of Birmingham was soon replaced by motorway as the school party headed towards the south coast and the Channel Tunnel. For some of the children it was their first time out of Birmingham, and for many their first time out of the country. Chrissie tried to distract herself from the enormity of what she was doing by chatting to Dan, who was sitting beside her, but it quickly became clear he had an agenda.

"When are you two going to patch things up?" he asked in a stage whisper.

"Who?" said Chrissie, playing for time. She knew exactly what he meant.

"You and Nisha. You've both been wandering around the school like a reception kid who misses her mum."

Chrissie sighed. "It's complicated."

"Blah blah, yeah yeah, stuff happened a hundred years ago and then there was some kind of fumble in the rain and now everything's weird. Is that about right?" he asked, folding his arms.

"What has she said to you?" asked Chrissie, surprised Nisha had shared anything about what had happened. The only person she'd told was Rae.

"Not much," said Dan. "She was looking a bit glum the other night after the staff meeting, so I took her for a pint. She wouldn't tell me the gory details, more's the pity."

Chrissie harrumphed. "I should hope not. Honestly, I don't know how all this became such a mess. What did you say to her?"

"I told her to just talk to you and sort it out. Pretty much what I'm saying to you now," he said, before turning in his seat and shouting, "I can smell prawn cocktail crisps being eaten. The regulations of this coach company stipulate that prawn cocktail crisps are not to be consumed before the hour of ten am. It is currently seventeen minutes past six, and I must therefore inform you that you are in breach." The coach had fallen silent. "Put them away, please." They heard rustling behind them, and then silence resumed.

"What the heck was that?" asked Chrissie.

"God I can't bear the smell, and definitely not at this hour of the day. Anyway, stop distracting me. Speak to Nisha. I think it may go better than you think."

"Well, it was actually her who shut things down last time," said Chrissie. "But we'll see."

A small voice emerged from behind them. "Miss Anderson, when we're in the tunnel, will we be able to see the fish swimming round above our heads?"

"Um, no, Hardev, the tunnel doesn't have windows, I'm afraid," said Chrissie, stifling a smile. Approximately fifteen children sighed in disappointment.

"But," added Nisha, a few rows back, "the cool thing about the train we go on in the tunnel is that the whole bus drives onto it, and we just stay here in our seats, prawn cocktail crisps notwithstanding."

A few children mustered an "ooh" in response.

"Yes," said Francis, who until now hadn't said a word. "And actually, the Channel Tunnel is fifty point five kilometres long and seventy-six metres deep, so putting windows in might compromise its structural integrity."

"Yes," said Dan, "that's exactly what I was about to say."

Chrissie jabbed him in the ribs. "Liar," she whispered.

"Who? Me? I'm affronted by the very suggestion," he replied with faux offence.

Chrissie allowed herself to drift off into thought as the miles sped by.

She remembered the morning Nisha had vanished from her garden. They'd been inseparable for weeks, so her unexplained absence alone was enough to confuse Chrissie. The fact that it had come after the night they'd shared together made it worse. Chrissie couldn't help wondering if she'd done something wrong.

Her dad was busying himself with builder's tea, complete with two sugars, when she stumbled into the house, shell-shocked.

"Did you see Nisha before she went?" she asked, her pyjama bottoms carrying dewy blades of grass into the kitchen.

"No, love, sorry. Everything ok?"

"Yeah, sure. I just didn't think she'd leave so early," said Chrissie, dropping her head to hide the tears that were threatening to fall from her eyes.

"I'm sure you'll sort it out, bab, whatever it is," he said. "I know how close the two of you are." He left the words floating in the air, concentrating his gaze on the teapot in front of him on the kitchen table. "And, well, if you ever wanted to tell me anything, you know you could." He paused. "Anything."

"There's nothing I need to tell you, Dad," said Chrissie, her voice breaking. She got the sense she'd been rumbled, but somehow that made it harder to admit that Nisha had just left without saying goodbye. After all they'd shared. "I'm going to have a shower."

Under the hot water, alone, she finally allowed herself to cry.

Chrissie loved her dad for wanting to help, and part of her wanted to tell him everything. But inside, she didn't know what that everything was. Her brain and body were bursting with excitement and passion and fear and anxiety. She felt full and empty all at once, and couldn't make sense of what had happened and why. If she couldn't explain it to herself, she definitely couldn't explain it to him. And while he had said she could tell him 'anything', did he really mean that? Did he really know what he was asking?

She waited in vain for Nisha to come back and explain herself. Maybe she'd just had to pop home for something and didn't want to wake Chrissie. But by lunchtime, there was no word, the phone hadn't rung, and Chrissie felt lost.

After a few days, Chrissie gathered all her courage and finally phoned Nisha's house. Her mum answered the phone, and after some muffled whispering, reported that Nisha was out. Chrissie didn't believe her. She was pretty sure she was being avoided.

The next time she saw her friend was at school on A

level results day, at the other end of the hall, where she spotted Nisha with her mum, gripping an envelope. Chrissie found her own envelope, but by the time she looked again Nisha was gone.

Chapter Twenty-Seven

"Are we nearly there yet?" asked Dan, echoing the whiny voices the children had been affecting in the last hour.

"Just a couple of miles to Folkestone," said Nisha. "Although I must admit, Le Shuttle on the coach is somewhat less civilised than the Eurostar. What I wouldn't give to be in the champagne bar in St Pancras right now!"

"I suspect this lot would ruin the vibe," said Chrissie, gesturing at the coachload who were at various stages of eating their packed lunches, even though it was still morning.

"Can I make a suggestion?" said Philippa. The teachers turned to look at the lawyer, who still seemed out of place on a coach full of primary school pupils, even after swapping her stilettos for a pair of designer white trainers. "Perhaps once we have crossed the border, we get an industrial quantity of baguettes and cheese and chocolate for those who've eaten their lunches too early." She narrowed her eyes at Dottie, who was among the guilty.

"Good plan," said Chrissie. "For now though, I think we need to get the passports sorted. It's going to be a nightmare getting through Customs, so the better prepared we are, the better it'll be for us."

In the end, it was less complex than they had feared. The officers were used to school trips, and Nisha and Chrissie's careful work meant they were ahead of the game.

The children were incredibly noisy in the tunnel, overexcited and sleep-deprived – the perpetual challenge of any school trip.

"Ok," said Philippa. "There's an Auchan supermarket in Coquelles, not long after we emerge on the other side. I'll speak to the driver and let him know we're stopping there."

"She's worth her weight in gold," said Nisha, standing next to Chrissie and Dan's seat and stretching her legs. "To say she's prepared is an understatement."

Dan put his thumbs up and Chrissie 'hmm'd in agreement, relieved that Nisha was being friendlier. She couldn't help but glance at her old friend's fingers. Her hands looked strong and capable, in a way that made Chrissie blush, and then berate herself for such unhelpful and inappropriate thoughts. She could imagine them holding her, touching her, feeling her. No, she had to stop this. This was not a route she was going down. Yes, Nisha was being friendlier, but clearly they weren't meant to be together – Chrissie had her rules, Nisha wasn't in the right place for it, and they had far too much history. Chrissie adjusted herself in her seat as the train began to slow.

The supermarket was an adventure. Many of the children needed the toilet, because that was the way of school trips. Chrissie and Nisha were sent into the Auchan while Philippa and Dan supervised in the toilet facilities, carefully counting heads at every stage.

"This reminds me of that trip we did to Berlin," said Nisha, as she and Chrissie grabbed baskets and walked down the well-stocked aisles of the large shopping outlet.

Chrissie remembered it too. "All the meat!" she exclaimed.

"Oh my God, yeah, they seemed to have no clue about vegetarianism back then," said Nisha with a laugh. "I think you survived on bread and chips."

"Yes, it was a very beige affair," replied Chrissie, wrinkling her nose. "Don't get me wrong, I love a bit of beige as much as the next person, but that was a bit much. My ex-wife would have existed exclusively on beige food, given the choice."

"Really?" asked Nisha, pausing and looking at Chrissie.

"Yeah," she said. "We always ate totally different things if we ate out together. We did a lot of things differently from one another, to be honest."

"A bit of an opposites attract thing?" asked Nisha, cautiously.

"I think so," said Chrissie. "Although we didn't always feel like opposites."

"Jake and I were always into all the same stuff," Nisha told her. "We both played football, we both taught in primary, we loved watching TV together." She grimaced slightly. "In the end, it was like we'd stopped having anything to talk about to each other because we were either doing the same things separately or doing them together." She dropped a selection of cheeses into her basket. "By the time the relationship had come to its end, we felt more like old friends than lovers. Any spark there might have been was long gone."

"That's sad," said Chrissie. "I'm sorry. Are you still

friends?" She couldn't help her curiosity about this great love of Nisha's life.

"Not sure, really." Nisha tugged at the toggle on her hoodie and looked at the floor. "I haven't really been in touch with him since I got here. What about you?"

"What? With Kiera? No, not really," said Chrissie, making a beeline to the long French loaves of bread. She mentally counted the children and adults and put ten batons in her basket. It seemed odd to be having such a personal conversation in a French supermarket, but at the same time, it was surprisingly easy. They walked along, side by side, chatting, safe in the knowledge that they were completely anonymous. "She keeps her distance, and to be honest, I really can't blame her. She saw the worst of me, and the me that wasn't really 'me' because of the cult, if you see what I mean."

"Yeah," said Nisha, "I get it. But perhaps you could be friends one day? It sounds like there were some good things about your relationship, at least."

"Not after what I did," said Chrissie, quietly. It was less a dramatic statement than one she felt was truthful and reasonable.

Nisha looked at Chrissie sympathetically, as she placed half a tonne of chocolate into her basket. "I can see how guilty you feel about it, and I can see how much you've changed your life because of it. Have you considered that maybe you need to forgive yourself?"

The pair walked towards the tills. "I think this conversation needs to wait until I've had a few glasses of wine," said Chrissie, smiling.

"Well," said Nisha, scooping up three bottles of red wine in her free hand, "that's a problem we can definitely fix."

Chrissie laughed. She loved it when things were easy between them like this.

Chapter Twenty-Eight

The school party were staying in a hostel on the outskirts of Paris. The children were hosted in five dormitories of bunk beds. It had taken over an hour to get each child into the right dorm and negotiate who absolutely had to be on the top bunk, and who was too terrified of heights to countenance the idea.

"Good heavens," said Nisha, flinging herself back on the bed in the twin room she was sharing with Chrissie. "Who knew bunk beds would be so controversial?"

"My favourite bit was when Francis pointed out that you could technically fall from the top bunk, break your neck and die," said Chrissie, unpacking her small suitcase into the tiny cupboard beside her single bed.

"Oh God," replied Nisha. "Did you see Dottie's face? If Philippa hadn't been there to shut her up, I don't know what we'd have done. I think Dottie's mum may become part of my classroom management technique."

"Tell that to her courtroom clients," said Chrissie with a laugh. "Hardev wasn't put off, was he? Trust him to declare he could dive off, land on his head and bounce right back up again!"

"Had to be Hardev, didn't it?" said Nisha, lying back with her head resting on her arms.

There was a knock at the door. "Oh no," said Chrissie, "tell me that's not one of the kids. I thought once we'd filled them with burgers and chips in the dining room downstairs they'd all settle down."

"It's only me," came a muffled voice. It was Dan.

"Come in," called Nisha, not moving from her spot.

The door opened. "Sorry, ladies," Dan said. "I have a poorly Francis." The pale boy was cowering behind him, looking as though he might vomit at any moment.

"Oh no," said Chrissie, walking over to take a closer look.

"I wouldn't get too close," said Dan. "We've had a couple of projectile moments, and I think another may be in the offing. Here," he added, picking up the waste paper bin at the door and handing it to poor Francis.

"Just when I thought we might get to settle down and chill for a bit," said Nisha under her breath.

"Have you ever been on a school trip before?" Chrissie admonished her. "Ok, Dan. What are we going to do?"

"Well, I can't leave him in the dorm – he'll vom everywhere and keep the other boys awake. I think we need to swap rooms. Philippa has the single and you two have the twin. My room has a double in it." Chrissie felt a knot forming in her stomach as Dan continued. "I need to stay with Francis, and if we stay in here, he can have a bit of space and access to your en-suite, and I can be in the bed on the other side of the room." He paused, and addressed his next comments to Nisha. "I realise it's not ideal, but if you two are happy to share a double, then we can all, hopefully, get a reasonable night."

There was a pause. Chrissie looked over at Nisha. "Sure," said Nisha, swinging her legs down from her bed and grabbing her bag. She hadn't unpacked yet. "Assuming Chris doesn't mind," she added, nodding her head towards Chrissie, but not making eye contact.

"Of course," said Chrissie, not knowing what else to say, but also certain this was not a good idea, on many levels.

The last time they'd shared a bed it had all ended in tears – most of them Chrissie's. As she gathered together her possessions and put them back in her bag, she reminded herself that that was twenty years ago. Ancient history. And anyway, she was a proper grown-up now, and she and Nisha appeared to have got over their troubles. She zipped up her bag. Yes, it would be fine.

"Are you going to be ok?" asked Nisha, looking at Dan and his tiny charge who was already retching into the bin.

"Sure," said Dan, dropping his bag on the floor by the bed Nisha had originally chosen. "I have supplies of the finest French lemonade, made by a lady called Stella Artois."

"Ah, got to love Stella. A bit of a harsh taste for me, but we've stocked up on grape juice made by Rio Cha," said Nisha.

Chrissie stifled a giggle as she patted Francis' back gently. "Will you be ok, Francis?"

"Yeah," he said, quietly. "Mr Harvey will look after me."

"He will," Chrissie told him with a smile. "Mr Harvey, give us a shout if you need help at any point."

Dan gave a thumbs up.

Chapter Twenty-Nine

"So," said Nisha, "it's certainly not a king-sized bed, is it?"

Chrissie stood beside her in the doorway of the room. "Nope. I mean, I'm not sure it's even a full double, if I'm honest. Do you want me to sleep on the floor?"

"What? No, that would be ridiculous. I'm sure this will be fine. We'll just have to keep very still to avoid knocking each other out," said Nisha, looking again at the tiny bed.

Chrissie could feel her heart in her throat, but couldn't work out why.

"Besides, it's not like we've never shared a bed before," said Nisha, looking at Chrissie for the first time since the double bed had been suggested. Chrissie couldn't work out whether that was a glint of amusement or annoyance in her eyes. She tried not to overthink it. She failed.

Chrissie sighed. "True," she replied, simply.

"Well, here we are. I think we've earned some wine," Nisha said, dropping her bag on the floor and pulling the promised bottle of Rioja from it.

"Ah yes, that Rio Cha grape juice," said Chrissie, sitting on one side of the bed. "You and Dan are a terrible influence on each other. And on me."

"Good," said Nisha, sitting beside her. "For what it's worth, I think you need a bad influence here and there."

Chrissie felt her stomach somersault in a way she hadn't felt since she'd kissed Nisha weeks ago. The kiss she had replayed in her head more times than she cared to admit, especially when Nisha grinned with that dimple of hers.

"I remain unconvinced," she said.

"Here," said Nisha, holding out a tiny toothbrush glass from the ensuite, filled with as much Rioja as it could house.

"What are you drinking from?" asked Chrissie, accepting the glass and taking a fulsome swig. She was going to need it.

Nisha held up the bottle. "See, ever the gentleman, letting you have the glass while I swig from the source." She poured the wine directly into her mouth and Chrissie laughed. It reminded her of the eighteen-year-old Nisha she remembered.

"Cheers," said Nisha.

"Your very good health," replied Chrissie. They both took generous mouthfuls and sighed.

"That's better," said Nisha. "I can't quite believe we're here."

"I know," said Chrissie.

"So, back to forgiveness, then." Nisha looked at Chrissie. The woman was relentless.

"Well, I guess I find it hard," said Chrissie, her edges beginning to soften with the wine. "Not only did I abandon Kiera like I've already told you, but it ended up being her who saved me. I mean, literally saved me."

"How do you mean?"

"The way it ended in Wales, I wound up hungry, cold and cut off from the world with a small group of others in the middle of nowhere in the Welsh hills. One day I saw Lucian's phone lying out on the side – he didn't let us have our phones. I knew I needed to get out, but I could only remember one number," said Chrissie.

"Hers," said Nisha.

"Yes. And she came, she rescued me and took me back to her place and gave me somewhere to stay for the first few weeks. I have no idea why she did, to be honest," said Chrissie, "but I know I couldn't have got away and started again without her."

"Wow." Nisha had shuffled closer to Chrissie, allowing their arms to touch. Chrissie felt a warmth spread through her at the contact. But she knew Nisha wasn't going to absolve her. No one could do that.

"So you can see why she would hate me. As it happens, I don't think she does. But she doesn't want to have anything to do with me, and I think that's about right. I wouldn't either. So I feel like forgiving myself is a long way off." Chrissie dropped her head, not sure what Nisha would do or say next.

"So you set yourself rules for the next part of your life to make sure you didn't mess up so badly again?" Nisha said. "For the first time, I sort of get it." She sighed. "This Kiera, she seems like she's actually pretty decent."

Chrissie felt a pain in her heart. "Yes, she is. And I think she's happy now, which I'm really pleased about."

"You don't want to get back with her?" asked Nisha.

"No," said Chrissie. "While I blew the relationship up in spectacular and damaging fashion, the truth is, we had stopped having anything in common. It wasn't working, and somewhere between Dad's death and meeting those people, I lost my way."

"And do you still do the poly thing?" asked Nisha.

"All the questions!" said Chrissie with a laugh, bringing a much needed dose of levity. "No. It all sounded wonderful and utopian, and I know there are people it works for. But in reality, it didn't work for me. I don't have anything against it. I think my friend Rae is poly, and they absolutely make it work. I'm quite envious, really. But I'm just not that person."

"Nah," said Nisha. "Me neither."

Chrissie could feel her friend's hand resting on hers. Such a light, gentle contact. But somehow, it felt like so much more.

Chapter Thirty

Butterflies fluttered up from Chrissie's stomach and her head swam slightly, thanks to the early start and the two glasses of wine she had imbibed. It wasn't an unpleasant sensation. "Right," she said. "Your turn. Tell me why you left after that night."

"I guess it's only fair," said Nisha. She puffed out a breath and looked up, to the artexed ceiling that owed its awful pattern to the nineties, along with the rest of the room's decor.

"Honestly, I think it is fair," added Chrissie, the wine emboldening her. "I can't tell you how lost I felt in that moment when I woke up and you were gone."

"I'm sorry," said Nisha. "Really, truly. I was sorry the moment I did it. But I couldn't help myself."

"Tell me about it." Chrissie's voice was barely above a whisper.

Nisha swallowed. "I remember waking up at about five. The birds were singing and I could feel the sun beginning to warm the tent. I looked over at you and you looked so perfect, lying there asleep, your golden hair spread about your head like a halo."

Chrissie looked at Nisha in surprise, but Nisha turned her face away before continuing. "It sounds stupid, I know. I just thought that this had been the most perfect twenty-four hours and the best night of my life, and whatever happened next would surely ruin everything."

"You wanted the fairytale?" said Chrissie, reaching out her hand and resting it on Nisha's thigh. Nisha twitched slightly, surprised by the touch.

Nisha turned to face Chrissie. "Yes. But more than that, I was afraid of what it all meant. If it became more than just a perfect twenty-four hours it meant that my life might end up entirely differently to the one I'd expected. Certainly different to what my parents expected."

Absentmindedly, Chrissie had begun to stroke her hand up and down Nisha's thigh, taking in the feel of the muscles beneath her fingers.

"It was twenty years ago," continued Nisha, "and I had no idea how to talk about the fact that I was in love with my best friend in a not-very-best-friend way. I wasn't afraid to be gay or bi or whatever, I just hadn't expected it, and I didn't know what to do." Nisha picked up the wine bottle and filled Chrissie's tiny glass for the last time, before taking another generous swig of the remaining Rioja. "And worst of all, I didn't know how to talk to you about it all."

"We could have worked it out together," said Chrissie, the words 'in love' swimming around her brain.

Nisha had said she was in love with her.

"Yes, and in hindsight, of course, that's what we should have done. But it didn't feel that way back then. It all felt so existential and I didn't know what to do. So I ran."

"You ran," said Chrissie. She drained her glass before speaking again. "Thank you for telling me."

Nisha gave a rueful smile. "And I know I've been an arsehole for the last few weeks. I'm sorry for that, too. I was ashamed of what I did, I guess a bit like you were with Kiera, so I pushed you away." She put her hand on top of Chrissie's.

"But not now?" said Chrissie, feeling her face drawn towards Nisha's as if by magnetism, feeling herself release her concerns.

"Not now," said Nisha. "I've been so miserable not talking to you properly." Her voice was soft, and Chrissie could feel her breath on her own face. "When really, all I've wanted to do was kiss you back since the moment you pushed me against that wall and planted your lips on me." Chrissie swallowed, her pulse quickening. "But I won't if you don't want me to. You made yourself clear before. You said you didn't want this." Nisha's dark eyes were trained on Chrissie's.

Chrissie adjusted the hand that was sandwiched between Nisha's hand and thigh, leaned forward, and this time, very softly and hesitantly, kissed the woman before her.

This time there was no Lucian, no rain, no drama. Just the two of them, a bottle of wine and the tiniest bed in human history. Nisha returned the kiss, and it felt different. It took Chrissie back to the tent for a moment or two, and then it changed, to the here and now. It was the Nisha she knew in this moment. The bold, honest, flawed Nisha who was a woman and was willing to own her actions.

Chrissie framed Nisha's face with her thumbs and deepened the kiss, allowing her tongue to brush her lips. Nisha sighed and put her arms around Chrissie, pulling her in closer. "You may well be the sexiest woman I've ever had the pleasure of kissing," she said, moving her face back slightly.

"Am I the only woman you've ever kissed?" asked Chrissie, suspicion in her voice.

Nisha laughed. "No. Not even slightly. I might have had a crisis back then, but I sorted myself out at uni."

"I bet you did," said Chrissie with a pout.

"Oh shut up and kiss me again, please," said Nisha, leaning back towards her colleague.

Chapter Thirty-One

Chrissie leaned forward and kissed Nisha again, this time with more confidence. She put her hand to Nisha's cheek, then pulled away slightly.

"Thank you," she said, simply.

"For what?"

"For telling me. I always wondered. I figured I'd never know. But then, I figured I'd never see you again." Chrissie's hand was still on Nisha's face.

Nisha gave a lopsided smile. "Well, I tend to get there. Eventually. I'm just sorry it took me so long. I always knew I'd done you wrong, but I never knew how to make up for it."

"I have an idea," said Chrissie, her cheeks reddening.

Nisha grinned. "Oh I think I know this one," she said. Gently, she pushed Chrissie back down onto the bed, then kissed her, while lowering herself down on top of her. "Is this ok?" she asked, pausing for a moment.

"Oh my God, yes," said Chrissie. "You have my full

consent." She pulled Nisha into her and felt her insides heat.

Nisha didn't need asking twice. She kissed Chrissie soundly, her tongue running along Chrissie's bottom lip. Chrissie took a sharp intake of breath, then sighed. She could feel her body responding to Nisha's touch in a way she hadn't felt for years. She could feel Nisha's muscular thigh pressing between her legs, giving their kisses a sense of urgency. She wanted more.

Nisha brushed her hand down Chrissie's side, then brought it back up, gently stroking her breast as she did.

"You've got moves," said Chrissie, her voice breathless.

"I didn't just study French at university, you know," said Nisha into Chrissie's neck, where she proceeded to apply her lips liberally.

"So I gather," said Chrissie, running her hands down Nisha's back, finding her bum and squeezing.

"Mmm," said Nisha. "I'm not the only one with moves."

Chrissie felt herself wanting more of the woman on top of her, wanting to give herself up in that moment. "God, you are so hot," she said, reaching down to pull Nisha's top up over her head. "Is this ok?"

"Chrissie, don't you know by now?" asked Nisha, sitting herself up to throw her top aside and look down at the other woman. "I want you. I always did." Chrissie felt something different now, something that was less about sex and more about… She wasn't sure what it was about, but it made her brain burst into orange flames. She decided not to think about what that meant.

Nisha leaned forwards and pulled Chrissie's top up, undoing her bra at the same time, and Chrissie helped.

There was a clumsiness to their urgency, but it was necessary.

"My goodness," said Nisha, looking down at Chrissie's skin, the pink of her nipples and the sweat glistening in her cleavage. "You are possibly the sexiest woman I have ever met."

Chrissie's eyes darkened. "Take off your bra," she instructed. Nisha didn't need telling twice, quickly removing the sports bra and flinging it across the room. She leaned back down, her breasts meeting Chrissie's, and they sighed in unison.

Chrissie put her hand on Nisha's hip and pushed her, flipping her onto her back. "Is this ok?" she asked, mirroring the question Nisha had put earlier.

"God yes," said Nisha, placing her hands on Chrissie's back, and enjoying the sensation of Chrissie's leg between hers.

They kissed in a mess of tongues and hands and arms and legs, in a way that made Chrissie wonder if she might climax before she'd even taken off her skirt. As if reading her mind, Nisha hooked her fingers under the waist band. "This needs to come off," she said, breathless.

"Only if you take off those jeans as well," said Chrissie.

"Deal."

Their clothes were efficiently abandoned, and they resumed their positions. Chrissie kissed Nisha's neck, earning a groan.

"I remember you liking that before," said Chrissie.

"You were the one who made me understand what I liked," said Nisha. "And that," she added in a gasp, as Chrissie ran her tongue over the dark brown nipple beneath her mouth. Chrissie smiled, but didn't stop kissing this woman. This woman she'd thought about for twenty years.

Chrissie had always wondered what meeting her again would be like, but she'd never considered the possibility of anything actually happening if they did. She drew her fingers up Nisha's smooth shin, over her knee, lingering over her toned thigh. "All that football," Chrissie sighed. She kissed Nisha's rounded stomach, feeling her lover squirm beneath her. "Be patient," she said, with a giggle.

"That's easy for you to say," said Nisha, but before she could say anything further, Chrissie had swept her tongue between her legs, over the cotton of her briefs.

"You were saying?" said Chrissie, popping her head up to look at the woman lying before her.

"Shut up and carry on doing that," replied Nisha, a hand gently resting on Chrissie's head. Chrissie laughed and swiftly used her fingers to pull the briefs to one side, so she could feel with her tongue how turned on Nisha was. Nisha groaned. Deftly, Chrissie removed the offending undergarment, before settling herself in a position where she could better access what she wanted – giving Nisha as much pleasure as she could.

Chrissie ran her tongue up through Nisha's centre, tasting how turned on she was, how ready she was. But she didn't want Nisha to climax so soon. Chrissie wanted to take her time and enjoy this. Twenty years ago they'd fumbled together, neither of them with any experience or understanding, just feeling their way. Now, she wanted to make sure that Nisha's every need and want was taken care of.

Chrissie continued to lick Nisha, slowly, deliberately, drawing her own pleasure from the sound of Nisha's moans. Chrissie could feel herself beginning to ache, wanting to be touched. She disengaged and moved, kissing Nisha on the mouth and replacing her tongue with her fingers. She could tell from the darkness of Nisha's eyes, from the way her mouth was set and her eyes were closed, that the time for teasing her was over. She pressed her first and then her second finger into Nisha, and her lover cried out.

"Shhh," said Chrissie in a stage whisper, "we're next door to Dan."

"And if you don't carry on doing that, I'll scream even louder," Nisha replied.

Chrissie grinned. She understood. She pushed into Nisha harder, enjoying the sight of the other woman's head thrown back, arms above her head, yielding completely to the moment. Slowly to start with, she pushed in and then out, in and then out, enjoying the feeling of Nisha's muscles squeeze her fingers.

Nisha's moans remained just quiet enough for Chrissie not to worry about Dan. She added her thumb, sweeping it over Nisha's most sensitive place.

"Oh God, yes," said Nisha, her face now turned into the pillow so as not to make too much noise, as she gave way to an orgasm Chrissie could see, hear and feel.

Chapter Thirty-Two

"I'm not the only one who's learnt a lot since the old days," said Nisha, when she'd finally regained the ability to form full sentences.

"Well, hello again," replied Chrissie. "I thought I'd lost you."

"Ha," said Nisha, rolling onto her side to face Chrissie. "Well, what can I say? You are exceptionally hot."

"Thank you," said Chrissie.

"And it's been a very long time since I did anything like that," added Nisha, earning a battering from a pillow from Chrissie.

"Charming," said Chrissie with a laugh.

"But in all seriousness, I think it's important we acknowledge that while I could collapse into a post-orgasmic reverie, it would be somewhat unfair to do so while you still have your knickers on."

Chrissie looked down at the polka dot underwear that she hadn't expected anyone to see. She smiled, and removed it. "Better?"

"Not quite," said Nisha, placing her hand onto Chrissie's shoulder before pushing her onto her back. "Did I tell you how beautiful you are?" she asked, her dark hair falling over brown eyes that somehow glittered in the half-light of the hostel room. Chrissie wondered how they'd ever worked together without doing this. Before she could complete the thought, she felt Nisha's strong hand caress her breast, and lost all rationality.

Chrissie grabbed Nisha's bum and pulled her in closer, needing to feel Nisha's weight on her. Nisha crushed Chrissie's lips with her mouth, her tongue touching Chrissie's.

Chrissie groaned and Nisha skated her fingers down Chrissie's front, grazing her nipples and traveling down between her legs. Firm fingers began a circular motion that soon had Chrissie breathless and desperate for more.

"Please," said Chrissie, unable to say anything more. Nisha nodded and moved her hand, pushing a finger inside Chrissie. "Yes," sighed Chrissie. "More."

Nisha continued, with a rhythm that Chrissie thought might send her into another dimension. Again and again Nisha moved, in such a way that Chrissie somehow felt her touch everywhere.

"I always wanted you," said Chrissie, before climaxing as quietly as she could, given the intensity of the moment.

In some ways, she thought, it was simply sex between co-workers away from home.

But she knew it was so much more.

Chapter Thirty-Three

"So sorry about last night," said Dan at breakfast. He looked slightly blearily at Nisha and Chrissie, who'd sat down opposite him, each studiously avoiding the other's gaze. "In the end Francis wasn't sick again, so it was all good. I didn't need to disturb you at all."

"Oh," said Nisha, "no, it's fine." Chrissie focused on her croissant.

"Obviously you can have your room back tonight," he continued.

"No!" said Chrissie, a little too quickly. "I mean, that's really not necessary."

"Er yes," added Nisha. "And you're a stinky boy and you've been a stinky boy in that bedroom now, so I don't want to get into your bed."

"Yes," agreed Chrissie, warming to the theme. "And I definitely don't want to get into Francis' sick bed."

"Good point," said Dan. "Sorry again," he said. "I know it's probably a bit weird for the two of you, sharing a bed."

"So weird," replied Nisha. "Just going to get another coffee." Chrissie glared at her back as she swiftly escaped the conversation.

"We made the best of it," said Chrissie, only very briefly allowing her eyes to meet Dan's. "Now, what's the plan for today?"

"Ah yes," replied Dan, as he picked apart a pain au chocolat. "Today is the Eiffel Tower. An absolute must-do, and I have the tickets all sorted already. God bless Philippa."

"Sorry, did I hear my name?" said Philippa from the doorway, her red lipstick by far the brightest thing in the room.

"Come and join us," said Chrissie, smiling at the woman who had become her class's unexpected hero.

"We were just talking about today's activities," Dan told her.

Philippa looked over at the children gathered around a long table on the other side of the room. "They look like they're muddling through ok."

"Yes," said Dan. "We had a few shenanigans about spreading margarine on toast, with several of the kids asking me to do it, but then Dottie and Hardev said they could do it and would willingly spread butter and jam on toast in exchange for sweets." He shrugged. "I'm not sure if they're taking advantage of their classmates or being enterprising, but I'm here for it."

Chrissie was laughing as Nisha returned. Chrissie was relieved the attention was no longer on them, and on how sleep-deprived she was sure they must look. That said, Nisha seemed to be glowing, her cheeks pink and her eyes wide and smiley. That dimple was doing its thing, and Chrissie was struggling to hide her own smile every time she saw it. She didn't know what was next for them, but she knew she felt good in a way she hadn't in such a long time. Rules or no rules, this was the right thing for them to do. She was sure of it.

Chrissie started on the pile of croissants Nisha had plonked in front of them. "Who knew school trips were so energy-sapping?" asked Nisha, her face the picture of innocence.

"They are the worst," said Dan, sighing. "But carbs will see us through. They always do."

Chrissie stifled a laugh before patting Dan's arm. "You'll be fine once you've had a coffee, sweetie. Besides, fruit and yoghurt is probably your best bet to perk you up. Carbs are good, but some healthy fat and plant matter will sort you right out as well."

"I see you've unleashed your inner hippy, then," said Nisha, giving Chrissie the side eye and squeezing her knee under the table where no one could see. Chrissie felt herself flush bright red and hoped no one had noticed.

"Yes," said Philippa, removing her cardigan, "it is a little hot in here. I'm quite pink myself." She looked at Chrissie sympathetically.

Chrissie hurriedly removed her own hoodie, nodding towards Philippa, who was clearly more observant than Dan. She felt Nisha's fingers on her knee again, and faked a coughing fit.

"You are terrible," said Chrissie, once she and Nisha were back in their room. "It's like you want everyone to know what we've been up to!"

Nisha laughed. "Is that such a bad thing?"

"No, of course not," said Chrissie, "not that we are, well," she struggled to describe what it was they were doing, "spending time together. But doing so on a school trip might not be ideal for our professional reputations."

"Fair," said Nisha. "Although I think I'd give it a stronger description than 'spending time together'." Nisha walked over to where Chrissie stood and pressed her against the door to their room.

"Also fair," agreed Chrissie. She looked at her watch. "But perhaps we can discuss that when we're not due at one of Europe's top locations with twenty-five children." She looked into Nisha's eyes, and found herself caring a little less about the children. When Nisha put her hand on Chrissie's waist, she breathed out and allowed Nisha to come in for a kiss.

"Ok," said Nisha, pulling away. "To be continued. But it *will* be continued."

Chapter Thirty-Four

The Eiffel Tower stood proud above the buildings and trees of its city, a remarkable feat of engineering from 1889 that was only ever meant to be temporary. Chrissie found it strange to imagine this landmark had watched over a city that had seen such turmoil and change in the last 135 years.

Their group was stood in a line across one of the bridges over the Seine, pausing so that anyone who wanted to could take a picture. Chrissie preferred just to look and take it in, while Nisha took about forty-seven photos and Dan made a short film for the school's Instagram channel.

"It's pretty impressive, isn't it?" said Philippa.

"It really is," said Chrissie.

"I've seen it countless times – my company has a sister branch here in Paris – but I am always taken aback every time."

"Your career sounds very glamorous," said Chrissie. "Not like ours." She gave a little laugh.

"No," said Philippa, "don't laugh. What you do is essential. Honestly, I cannot tell you how much you have given Dottie this year." Philippa looked over at her daughter, who was pointing out a blue boat to her friends. "She had terrible anxiety last year, but somehow between you and Ms Rajan, you seem to have helped her find some calm." She sighed. "I know she seems confident and chatty, but we had some really tough times last year. Her father is away a lot on business, for weeks at a time, and she struggles when he's not there, worrying about him being ok. The irony is that he's almost always in a first class lounge or five star hotel somewhere, so he's more than ok…" Her voice trailed off, making Chrissie wonder how Philippa felt about her husband being absent so much of the time.

"It must be hard for you both," said Chrissie, carefully.

"Oh, not for me," replied Philippa with a laugh. "To be honest, I'm not sure what I'll do when he retires. He's been working like this for the last seventeen years." She gazed along the Seine. "We've always lived separate lives, to be honest."

Chrissie thought back to her own marriage. She could relate. But she knew that for some people, that sort of relationship worked.

"But back to you," said Philippa. "Have you ever thought about training to be a teacher? You seem eminently capable, and I'm sure you'd be accepted onto a course."

"Oh, I'm not sure really," replied Chrissie, shrugging it off. "I need to work to pay my rent. Taking time out of work to train would be tricky." Working at the school had been part of her desire to give something back. She'd never thought about what it might give to her.

"Perhaps you should consider it," said Philippa, giving Chrissie a hard stare.

"Mmm," replied Chrissie, not sure where to put herself.

"Ms Rajan, I think perhaps it's time to move onto the tower?" she said, raising her voice and changing the subject.

Nisha waved from the other end of the group of children, and Chrissie's heart leap as an involuntary – and thoroughly indecent – image from the night before flashed across her mind. "Come on, everyone," said Nisha, "time to rock and roll." The children began to shuffle towards the Eiffel Tower, chattering loudly about how scared or otherwise they were of the height they might end up climbing to.

"I could climb to the very top and sit on the point without being scared," Hardev announced.

"Right you are, mate," said Dan. "Come on, you lot, pick up your feet."

Happily, because they were a pre-booked group, the Birmingham school party didn't have to wait in the enormous queue filled with tourists from around the globe. For the sake of simplicity, and to keep things interesting for the children – and perhaps to tire them out a bit – they'd opted to take them up the stairs rather than use the lift.

By the time they'd all reached the main platform, they were ready for a rest. "Ok, everyone," said Nisha, "grab your water bottles and have a little drink before you do anything else, please."

Suddenly, the sound of Nisha using her teacher voice had become something far more intimate to Chrissie, who had been bossed about by the teacher in a very different setting just a few hours earlier. She shook her head. This was not the time.

"Miss Anderson?" came a little voice. It was Francis. "I'm a bit scared. Will you hold my hand?" Chrissie looked down at the boy, who had significantly more colour in his cheeks than he'd had the night before.

"Of course, Francis. It is very high, isn't it?" said Chrissie. His hand was cold. "Don't you have gloves?"

"I have mittens," Francis replied, "but Hardev said they were babyish." He looked at his shoes.

"Mittens!" said Chrissie, "I love mittens. Look at mine," she added, pulling her purple and green woollen ones from her pockets. "These are my favourite pair. Look, I've got them on now, and I'm not a baby, am I?"

"No," said Francis, a smile forming on his face. "Look, mine are blue and red." He put them on.

"Lovely," Chrissie told him. "I must get a pair like that."

It was clear Francis wasn't going to cope with the higher levels of the tower, so Chrissie offered to stay behind with him while Dan, Philippa and Nisha took the rest of the overexcited rabble up.

"Right, Francis. Don't tell anyone, but as well as mittens, I love hot chocolate. There's a café over there, and I think they do hot chocolate with cream and marshmallows on. What do you think?" asked Chrissie, once the rest of the children had disappeared.

Francis' eyes grew large. "Are we really allowed?"

"Yes," said Chrissie, looking at his tiny frame and thinking he could probably use the calories. "Come on, let's go."

They sat side by side, drinking their hot chocolate and studiously avoiding the view in case it made Francis feel afraid. Chrissie allowed herself to think back to the feel of Nisha's lips on hers, Nisha's hands on her body, and shivered. The sweetness of the hot chocolate only added to the sensation of warmth she was experiencing.

"Miss," said Francis, taking her from her reverie. "I think this hot chocolate and the mittens have made me brave enough to look at the view now."

"Wow," said Chrissie. "Ok, Francis, if you're sure."

"I'm sure. But perhaps you could hold my hand?" he suggested. "But don't tell the others."

"Deal," said Chrissie with a smile.

Chapter Thirty-Five

The next stop was Notre Dame Cathedral, but getting the children there via the Batobus Boat was something of an adventure.

Chrissie spent most of the journey with Francis and another child, who both felt sick on the journey. Meanwhile, Nisha was chatting away with the more confident children alongside Philippa, and Dan was searching for Hardev, who had declared he was off to speak to the driver. Chrissie felt her eyes starting to close with the gentle bobbing of the passenger vessel. Her two charges were gazing into the paper bags they'd been issued.

She sighed. Paris was a wonderful city, but perhaps less romantic when there was a schedule that had to be followed to the letter, and when she and Nisha were surrounded by children and well-meaning adults. She knew the two of them probably needed to talk, but this wasn't the place for that.

Chrissie felt restless. Bored, even, of being responsible for the children. Being with Nisha had released something in her, reminded her of the person she'd once been. She wondered whether Nisha had been right when she said the rules she had made for herself were too strict, whether she had set her life up to be too controlled. The freedom she had felt with Nisha the night before felt life-changing.

She laughed at herself. It was one night. How much could it change her life?

Once they reached Notre Dame, they unloaded the children and gathered them on the steps in front of the cathedral to eat their packed lunches. These had been issued by the hostel they were staying in – twenty-nine white paper bags, containing cheese rolls, crisps and apples.

"Mum," said Dottie, loudly, "what if someone here was vegan? What would they eat?"

"Darling," Philippa replied, "no one here is vegan, so we don't need to worry."

"But what if they were?"

"What if the moon were made of cheese?" asked Dan, stepping in to redirect Dottie's inquisition, which had been aimed squarely at her mother for the past two hours.

"Well that's ridiculous," said Dottie. "Only nursery children think the moon is made of cheese."

Nisha looked over at Chrissie and gave her a smile. Chrissie replied with a half-smile of her own, frustrated the pair couldn't escape to a pavement café and spend time together over a carafe of wine. Nisha twisted her eyebrows. "Are you ok?" she mouthed.

"Yeah," said Chrissie, standing to walk over to her friend. "Just a bit tired, and I could do with some non-child time."

"Why don't you take a couple of minutes to yourself?" said Nisha, quietly. "These guys are all busy working out who has the best flavoured crisps and the reddest apple, they'll be occupied for a while yet. We've got it."

"Are you sure?" asked Chrissie, her heart lifting. A little time to process everything that had happened might do her good. Nisha nodded firmly, and Chrissie smiled gratefully.

She strolled away from the cathedral towards a row of cafes and shops, and without realising precisely where she was heading, found herself standing outside a bookshop – Shakespeare and Co. She remembered reading about this place, a famous stockist of English language books that had been in the city since the 1920s. James Joyce had been a frequent visitor in his early days. Yes, this was exactly the kind of place she could escape to.

It had been a long time since Chrissie had allowed herself to do something entirely selfish, but now she had begun to question her own rules, perhaps this was the time. She went into the shop, which was stuffed full of all kinds of books on ancient higgledy-piggledy shelves.

The shop's walls were lined with books from floor to ceiling, and in some places the ceiling was double height, with small landings overlooking those browsing the stock on the ground floor. It felt like a magical space, filled with people who enjoyed the freedom reading offered.

Chrissie went upstairs to one of the mezzanines, where she quickly found a book that was intended to be read in the shop, rather than sold. She pulled up a chair and settled herself down to read about Joyce's Paris adventures and his journey to publishing *Ulysses* there, in a bid to overcome the censors. She lost herself in the smell of the musty pages, the words packed onto the paper and the dreamy environment of the shop.

It wasn't until she'd finished one of the lengthy chapters in the book that she realised the time. She'd left her phone on silent, and had eight missed calls from Nisha and Dan. A few minutes had turned into an hour, and they wanted to know where she was.

Chrissie swore at herself, closed the book and hurried out of the shop. She trotted over the cobbles, dashing towards the cathedral.

"I'm so sorry," she said to Nisha as she hurried towards the cluster of children admiring the rebuilt spire of Notre Dame as they listened to a tour guide.

Nisha's mouth was in a straight line. "We've lost Hardev," she said under her breath. "Dan's gone to look for him, so it's just been me and Philippa and this lot." She motioned her hand towards the children.

"God, I'm sorry. Do you need me to go and help Dan?" Chrissie felt the hot sensation of guilt flood her, something she hadn't experienced for a while.

"No," said Nisha, failing to hide the annoyance in her voice. "I need you here. While I could have predicted Hardev would go walkabout at some point, I didn't expect you to. Where the hell did you go?"

"Sorry," said Chrissie, knowing that the actual answer wouldn't help matters. "Look, I'll make it up to you."

"You'd better," replied Nisha, her face grim. Her dimple was nowhere to be seen. "And text Dan to let him know you're back here."

Chrissie did as she was asked, before walking over to a small group of boys who seemed to be trying to drift off towards the river. "Come on, you lot, stay with the group, please," she said, wishing more than anything that she could just go straight to bed and have a little cry and a sleep.

Chapter Thirty-Six

"Where on earth was he?" asked Nisha, looking round to see Dan approaching with a slightly pale-looking Hardev in tow.

"He was trying to flag down a police boat on the Seine. He thought they might give him a ride," said Dan.

Nisha rolled her eyes, while Chrissie looked on and concentrated on trying not to annoy her colleagues any further. "Of course, why wouldn't he?"

"Well," said Dan, "me and Hardev have had a very grown-up conversation about how serious this is, and what could have happened."

"Quite right, Mr Harvey," agreed Nisha, fixing Hardev with a hard stare. Hardev's eyes grew large, and he turned to Chrissie, who gave him a sympathetic look. She knew how he felt.

"Ah, Miss Anderson, nice to have you back," said Dan, noticing her presence. "I hope you managed to get that important job done." He gave her a wink – clearly not as annoyed as Nisha was.

"Er yes," said Chrissie. "It took a little longer than I thought it would. Sorry I was away so long."

Dan gave her a quick smile, before ushering Hardev back into the group of children.

"Right," said Dan, "the Louvre?"

"Oui, bien," agreed Philippa with a smile. She appeared to have remained utterly unflappable since the start of the trip, in spite of all the children had thrown at them so far.

"Lovely," said Dan, opening up his phone to check the walking route.

"It's across the Pont Saint-Michel, I think," said Philippa, her mental map of Paris clearly quite comprehensive.

"Allons y!" announced Dan, organising the children into a crocodile.

"Do I have to stand with Hardev?" whined Dottie.

"Yes," said Nisha. "I need you both up front with me, showing me which way to go. Francis, are you ok over there? Yes, you walk with Erin. Perfect."

Chrissie found herself a place near the middle of the group, while Dan and Philippa brought up the rear. She had the sense it might be helpful to give Nisha a bit of space. She could tell she was annoyed with her. She ached to get back to the hostel where her journal was. She hadn't written in it since the previous day, and so much had happened. The window of freedom and joie de vivre she had opened up in the last twenty-four hours had suddenly closed back down.

The rules were there for a reason. She had messed things up.

Chapter Thirty-Seven

Nisha was sitting on the edge of the bed, organising her pyjamas – pyjamas she hadn't worn the night before. Chrissie looked at her back, her heart pounding and her stomach heavy.

"Sorry," said Chrissie. It was the first time they'd been alone together since that morning. "I know I messed up."

"You really did," said Nisha. "What was that all about?" She continued to focus her attention on the hem of her green pyjamas.

Chrissie walked around and sat beside Nisha, desperate to create some kind of connection between them. She considered placing her arm against Nisha's, but thought better of it. "Remember how you said I was too buttoned up, that I'd repressed part of myself?"

Nisha looked up for the first time, making brief eye contact.

"Well," Chrissie continued, "after last night, I felt like life had possibility again. That maybe, the time had come to set aside my rules. It felt so freeing. And that's because of you."

"I get that," said Nisha, "and I'm thrilled to hear it. Although, by the way, this is all you. You have the power to live your life the way that suits you best. But what about disappearing?"

"I just lost myself in that bookshop, reading and thinking and luxuriating in the space. I felt like I was somehow part of it, like I was essential to its being," Chrissie sighed. She knew she wasn't expressing herself the way she wanted to.

"You were at one with the bookshop?" said Nisha, a sarcastic tone to her voice that made Chrissie want to cry.

"No, no, I'm not articulating myself well. Sorry. I mean I just lost myself there. I started reading all about the history of the place and I could feel all the possibility of my life opening up. And I forgot about everything else," said Chrissie, looking at the shabby chest of drawers against the wall in front of her.

"You forgot about us. I see," said Nisha, her lips pursed.

Chrissie could feel her heartbeat, an echo of the way it had thumped when her ex-wife couldn't seem to understand her excitement at chakra dancing. It hurt. "And this is why I have the rules," she said, her voice low.

"Because you have a tendency to lose yourself," said Nisha. Chrissie nodded. "Hmm. I see. I guess that makes sense." Nisha sighed. "Might there be a middle way? Couldn't you allow yourself happiness and freedom without getting in too deep and forgetting everyone around you?"

"I really don't know," Chrissie replied. There was a silent pause. Nisha stood up with her pyjamas and walked to the bathroom to get changed.

Chapter Thirty-Eight

Chrissie woke early next morning, and decided to get herself ready and go down to breakfast. She couldn't bear the coldness she could feel emanating from Nisha, and snuck out of their room before her companion awoke.

The heap of pain au chocolat and jugs of fresh coffee were just what she needed to start the day. She had just enough time for a small cup and a pastry before going to rouse the children. Hopefully it would give her the space to gather her thoughts.

Chrissie took her journal from her bag, wondering where to start. She took a sip from her coffee and began to write. She began with the bookshop, then moved onto Nisha's dimple, that night and then the coldness that had returned to their tempestuous relationship. She revisited her rules. She had abandoned all three, at least partially.

Rule 1 – don't fall in love. She put a giant question mark next to that one. She wasn't in love, was she? She was in something, but she wasn't sure what. Something that made her heart ache and her blood pound and her brain race.

Lust? No, that sounded tawdry. This was more than that. Whatever it was, she definitely wasn't sticking to the letter of Rule 1.

Rule 2 – question everything. Well, she was certainly questioning everything now. But should she have questioned things earlier? Should she have questioned herself and where things were going when she was kissing Nisha? Should she have questioned her desire to escape from the school trip? Quite possibly. But as she remembered that kiss, that night, she felt her skin heat and the hairs on her arms stand up. Her head might be questioning it, but it was clear her body had no doubts.

What did that even mean?

Rule 3 – give back. She'd abandoned that the moment she had thought of herself above her colleagues – her friends – and disappeared into the reverie of the bookshop. Hardev might never have gone missing if she hadn't gone for so long. She had been stupid and selfish. She berated herself internally.

Chrissie finished the last crumbs of her pain au chocolat, packed away her notebook and climbed back upstairs. She went straight to the dormitories and knocked loudly, shouting "wakey wakey" to the children, most of who were very much awake already.

She opened the door to one of the dorms. "Come on, Francis, I know you're tired, but you'll perk up no end once you've had one of those giant pancakes. I think there's still some Nutella left after you and Dottie attacked it yesterday morning," Chrissie said with a laugh. Francis hopped out of bed. "Ok, everyone, get yourselves dressed and washed. And Hardev, please brush your teeth this time." She closed the door on a hubbub of activity, and turned to see Nisha in the hallway, having just done the same job with one of the other rooms.

"Morning," said Nisha levelly. "Dan and Philippa have done the other rooms, so all the kids should be ready to eat soon." She smoothed down her freshly showered hair. "I missed you this morning."

"Oh, I couldn't sleep past six, so I went down and had a sneaky quiet breakfast to myself." Chrissie kept her voice light, relieved Nisha seemed less annoyed this morning.

"Look," said Nisha, her eyes screwed up, "I think I was a bit harsh yesterday."

"I can understand why," said Chrissie, her voice low, not wanting any wagging ears to hear their conversation.

"I know. I just think that perhaps I took it all a bit too personally. I mean, given what I did to you all those years ago, just disappearing," Nisha trailed off. "I just think I need to keep this in proportion."

"For what it's worth," Chrissie told her, leaning back against the hallway wall, "I think you were right. I got wrapped up in myself, and I shouldn't have done that."

"But don't we all, sometimes?" said Nisha. Chrissie felt some of the weight that had been on her chest begin to lift.

"Maybe," said Chrissie. She was desperate to continue the conversation, but at that moment Philippa joined them in the hallway, followed closely by Dan.

"Now all we have to do is wait for that horrible lot to put their clothes on," said Dan with a sleepy smile. Chrissie smiled back in his direction. He was so unrelentingly positive and kind. She was grateful for his presence on this trip. He seemed to take everything in his stride. She wished she could be more like that.

"Well if any of you see Dottie wearing that Taylor Swift

T-shirt on again, I'd appreciate it if someone could let her know it's rank and she needs a clean top today," said Philippa. "I'm trying not to helicopter parent her while we're here, as she needs to experience the trip like all the other children, but my goodness, if I have to look at that chocolate stain down the front one more time, I may well lose my mind."

"On it," said Nisha with a chuckle. "And you know what, good for you for taking a step back. I don't think a lot of parents would manage it."

"It's good for her," said Philippa. "Her dad's away so much, we live in each other's pockets. It can be a bit like being a single parent at times." She adjusted her hair. "Don't get me wrong, most of the time it's absolutely fine. But sometimes…"

"I get you," said Chrissie, "I get like that towards the end of term."

"I get like that one week into term," added Nisha, and they all laughed. A door opened. "Go and change your top, Dottie," said Nisha, as the children started filing out into the corridor.

Chapter Thirty-Nine

"Francis," said Dan, "I think you need to eat your ice-cream a little quicker than that. It might be November but you've taken so long it's melting all over your fingers."

The children were in the Jardins de l'Avenue Foch beside the Arc de Triomphe, where those with smartphones had flattened their batteries by taking hundreds of pictures of the giant monument and the Champs-Elysees.

It was an unseasonably warm day in Paris, and a delegation of the class had presented themselves to Dan – by far the softest touch – and requested ice-creams. Chrissie suspected Dottie had been behind it, as she had piped up with the fact that she knew how to order ice-cream in French, and wouldn't it be a good way for them to practice their language skills?

Nisha and Chrissie sat with Philippa on a bench, soaking up the sun. They had opted for coffees to pep them up after another long day of walking around Paris with a class full of children.

The sun felt warm on Chrissie's face in spite of the chilly wind, and it gave her hope. Perhaps things would be ok.

"Thanks, Philippa," said Chrissie. "We would never have been able to do this without you."

"Oh, don't thank me," replied the woman, as immaculately dressed as always. "It was the company. It was just a bonus I could get involved. Well, a bonus for me, at least."

"And for us," said Nisha, flashing her best smile at the woman, piquing Chrissie's jealousy at the same time.

"Well thank you," said Philippa. "I've actually really enjoyed it. It's been hard work, of course it has. But being around you two and Daniel has been really lovely. You're all so friendly." She sipped from her macchiato. "I'm not really close to anyone I work with, and most of the rest of the time I'm with Dottie, so I don't have loads of friends."

"Well," said Nisha, throwing an arm loosely around Philippa's shoulder, "you have us now." She put her other arm around Chrissie. "Doesn't she, Chris?"

"You do," Chrissie beamed, feeling her heart quicken at Nisha's touch, which was somehow enjoyable at the same time as it was confusing.

"But I'm not going to lie, I could do with a night in my own bed," added Philippa with a laugh. "Those hostel beds aren't the best, are they?"

Nisha coughed before answering, squeezing Chrissie's shoulder. "No, I barely slept a wink the first night."

Chrissie was grateful that they were sitting side by side so Philippa couldn't see how red her face had gone. She thought about the forthcoming evening, and her heart dropped slightly. She wondered if kissing Nisha again, being with her again, was a risk she could afford to take, given what had happened the day before.

"Ah well," said Chrissie. "Time to go back to the hostel for tea, and then we'll be up bright and early tomorrow for our trip back to Birmingham. Is it wrong that I'm actually looking forward to the sight of Spaghetti Junction?"

Nisha laughed.

Philippa's phone rang. "Oh," she said, surprised. "It's Paul, my husband. Sorry, I should take this." She stood and walked away from their bench.

"I get the sense that Paul doesn't really appreciate her," said Nisha under her breath.

"No," Chrissie agreed, "but I suppose we all have different expectations of relationships, and different ideas of what works. She seems like she has everything worked out."

"Yeah. She seems lonely, though," said Nisha.

"Hmm. Maybe. Well, like you said, she has us now. I know we don't normally make a habit of being friends with parents, for completely sensible reasons, but I feel we can trust her."

"I agree," said Nisha. A few moments later, Philippa came back over and sat back down, her face a little pale.

"Are you ok?" said Chrissie.

"Er, yes. I think so, at least. Nothing major, it's just a bit of a shock, really. Paul's been made redundant." Philippa sounded like she could hardly believe the words she was saying. "As of now. He's flying back to the UK tomorrow morning, he'll be home by the time I get in tomorrow afternoon."

"Wow," said Nisha, "that's a lot."

"Yes," said Philippa, her mouth a straight line. "Right, I think we need to get this lot back to the hostel before the sugar rush turns into a slump and they all turn into monsters." She stood up and started gathering the children, even though they had at least twenty minutes before they needed to go anywhere.

Nisha and Chrissie looked at one another quizzically.

The group made its way slowly through the streets of Paris, pausing for a last look at the Eiffel Tower. "It's beautiful, isn't it?" said Chrissie, as much to herself as to Nisha.

"It is," said Nisha, leaning on the bridge beside her, admiring the landmark. The children were busy chatting to one another, sharing the sweets they'd all inevitably bought in a nearby gift shop, and discussing their favourite part of the trip. The two women felt unseen.

Standing side by side on the bridge, watching the boats going by on the Seine, Chrissie felt Nisha lean almost imperceptibly towards her. Their arms touched and rested together. Chrissie closed her eyes for a moment, savouring the contact. The backs of their hands brushed, and Chrissie looked over at Dan and Philippa, who were engaged in an animated discussion with some of the children, paying them no attention. She allowed herself to look at Nisha, who smiled at her.

"Fancy being in the most romantic city in the world," said Nisha, "and being with this lot."

"Ha ha, yeah, they are something of a mood killer," admitted Chrissie.

Nisha lowered her voice. "Because if we were alone right now, I would kiss you right here on this bridge under the Eiffel Tower."

Chrissie gripped Nisha's fingers between her own, briefly, her heart fluttering as she imagined that kiss. Other parts of her began to awaken too. But she knew she couldn't get lost in the moment. She had to keep herself anchored. If she'd learned nothing else, that was essential. She couldn't give herself over to Nisha entirely.

"Mr Harvey says you two need to stop mooning at the tower and come with us to the hostel," said Dottie, who had appeared beside them. Chrissie abruptly broke contact with Nisha's hand and looked over at Dan, who gave her a wink.

So much for them keeping things stealthy.

Chapter Forty

Dinner that evening was pasta, and the children fell upon it like they'd not eaten their own bodyweights in ice-cream and sweets.

Chrissie, Philippa, Dan and Nisha had decided to sit on a table slightly away from the children. They seemed in good spirits, after all, and the food was taking up most of their attention.

"So, how long have you two been together?" asked Philippa, her eyes laser-focused on Nisha and Chrissie.

"Together?" echoed Nisha.

"Us?" said Chrissie, unsure of what to say or how to handle this. They hadn't even decided for themselves what they were, or indeed if they were anything beyond colleagues with a complicated past.

"Lose the act, Anderson," said Dan under his breath. "We saw you holding hands on the bridge."

"Ugh," said Nisha. "Is nothing sacred?"

"Nope," said Dan.

"Well, I think we can all agree, what happens on school trip, stays on school trip," said Nisha. Chrissie wondered what that meant. Was this just a one-time thing? Would that be so bad? Perhaps Nisha had just wanted a bit of fun, to revisit the past?

"Well I think you make a wonderful couple," said Philippa, who had more colour in her cheeks than she'd had earlier in the day. "You've obviously got a lot in common, you've got a great working relationship, and I can see you've enjoyed being in this wonderful city." She smiled. Chrissie smiled back, not wanting to reveal how many questions she still didn't have answers to. She felt Nisha's hand squeeze her knee, which calmed her busy brain.

"Why thank you," said Nisha. "But in the meantime, should someone make sure Francis eats some actual food and not just tomato ketchup?" Chrissie stood up and headed over to the children's table, grateful to Nisha for changing the subject.

After the children had settled reluctantly down for bed, Nisha and Chrissie rejoined Dan and Philippa in the dining room. Dan conjured up a couple of bottles of wine, and poured each of them a liberal glass.

"Here's to surviving the trip in one piece," said Dan, holding up his glass.

"Don't speak too soon," said Nisha. "We still have to get them onto the coach and back to England, and some of those little guys have form."

"Very true," said Dan, "which is why I personally will be keeping both of my eyes on Hardev at every opportunity. He's not escaping this time."

Chrissie reddened. "Yes, apologies, that was a bad time to disappear."

Dan waved his hand. "We've all done it," he said. Nisha squeezed her hand under the table. Chrissie relaxed slightly. "And anyway, I figured you were probably a bit distracted," he added with a wink.

"What?" said Chrissie.

Philippa smiled at Dan, who continued. "Well, given that it's down to me that you're now 'a thing'," he used air quotes, "you should really be thanking me."

Nisha rolled her eyes. "Oh yes? And how exactly is this down to you?"

"If I hadn't gallantly given you my room so I could attend to a puking child, you'd have been like Victorian school ma'ams in separate beds," he said.

"Dan!" said Chrissie, her cheeks pink.

"But instead, I fell on my sword, saw to the diseased child, and gave you the opportunity of a lifetime."

"Really, Dan?" said Nisha.

"So it's understandable that you were away with the fairies yesterday," continued Dan, ignoring all warnings. "You, Chrissie, were drunk on lust."

"Oh my God," spluttered Chrissie, putting down her wine glass. "Stop it now!"

Philippa laughed, and soon they were all giggling. Chrissie looked over at Nisha, whose head was thrown back in mock incredulity.

"Anyway," said Dan, "we have an early start tomorrow and I need to pack my things." He stood up and drained his glass.

"Yes, me too," said Philippa, quickly following suit.

Once they had gone, Chrissie felt Nisha's hand squeeze her knee. "So, do you want to pack your things?" she asked, a teasing note to her voice.

Chrissie felt a shiver travel up her thigh. "I really, really do," she replied in a low voice.

"Excellent," said Nisha, pulling her up by the hand and leading her to their room.

Chapter Forty-One

Nisha locked the door behind them and pushed Chrissie against the wall.

"I thought we were packing our cases," said Chrissie, her eyes wide.

"Shut up," replied Nisha, with a giggle, before covering Chrissie's mouth with her own.

Chrissie moaned, enjoying the sensation of being pressed against the wall. She felt Nisha's hands explore her waist, her hips, her breasts. She kissed back harder. "It's going to be murder waking up early in the morning," she said, breathless.

"I don't care," said Nisha, pulling Chrissie's top off and undoing her bra with one hand.

"Skills," Chrissie observed, genuinely impressed. It was a three-clasp bra, and usually took her a couple of attempts to undo.

"Thank you," said Nisha, before bending her lead to kiss Chrissie's breasts, causing her to moan even more.

Meanwhile Chrissie was busy tugging Nisha's hoodie

and sweatshirt over her head and throwing it on the floor. She enjoyed the feel of Nisha's bra pressed against her naked torso. She lowered her hands and squeezed Nisha's bum.

"You are so much sexier than I remember," said Nisha, "and I always thought you were sexy back then." She gasped as Chrissie pushed her hands down into her jogging bottoms and pants, cupping her bottom.

Nisha pulled back slightly to undo Chrissie's jeans. There was something pleasing about the sound of the zip as she pulled it down. Chrissie smiled and pulled Nisha back to her for a long, deep kiss.

Nisha used both hands to loosen Chrissie's jeans, before plunging one hand into her knickers, feeling for herself how turned on her partner was. "Oh God," said Chrissie, feeling the ease with which Nisha's fingers slid into her. For a moment she thought her legs would buckle, and it took all her concentration to stand firm.

Nisha brought her head to Chrissie's neck and gently kissed her tender skin there, while Chrissie threw her head back, biting her lip to keep from calling out. "Yes," she whispered as Nisha curled her fingers at just the right angle. She grabbed Nisha's waist and pulled her nearer, filled with a need to feel so close it was like the other woman was part of her. "Don't stop," she begged under her breath.

"I will never stop," said Nisha. "Never," and at that moment Chrissie had what she thought was the most intense orgasm she had ever experienced. She ignored her shaking legs and how hard she was biting her lip, as all her nerve-endings seemed to align in one perfect moment of pleasure.

Seconds later she stood, still pinned to the wall by Nisha, limp and breathing hard. "Wow," she said.

"You look like you need a lie down," said Nisha with a snigger.

Chrissie laughed. "I do. But I am absolutely not in need of sleep right now. I have plans for you."

"I should damn well hope so," Nisha replied. She smiled, and took Chrissie's hands, leading her to the bed.

"How did we get here?" asked Chrissie, looking at the bed, their surroundings.

"Well, that orgasm was even better than it looked," said Nisha.

"No, stupid," said Chrissie. "I mean, all those years ago. Can you imagine telling those girls that twenty years later we'd be here, like this?"

"No, I really can't," said Nisha. "For a start, I think I would have been too scared to think about what the future held. That was my problem back then. Perhaps always my problem. I think Jake felt a bit like that when I left London – like I couldn't face a different kind of future there." Nisha stared at the ceiling for a moment. "Sorry, you don't want to hear about my ex, and definitely not here, in this moment."

"It's ok," Chrissie told her. "We've all got a past. I mean, you know about mine. None of us are perfect. Far from it."

"Very true," said Nisha. "Like now, for example, you still have your jeans and knickers on."

"And you're still wearing your bra and joggers," laughed Chrissie.

"Well I think this can be easily resolved, no costly therapy required."

Chapter Forty-Two

In a bid not to make it all too obvious, Chrissie sat next to Philippa on the coach home.

"How are things with your husband?" asked Chrissie, remembering how pale and quiet Dottie's mum had been the previous day. She was a little better today, but still seemed to have lost something.

"Oh, well, just the same, really. He's currently winging his way back home," said Philippa, fiddling with her phone. She seemed unusually distracted.

"Are you worried about money?" asked Chrissie, keen to know why Philippa seemed so out of sorts.

"Oh no, nothing like that. We're lucky in that respect. I guess it's just that I've got used to my life being like this. Just me and Dottie and work. Yes, it's been lonely, but it's going to be quite a shift to have Paul back home again. It's been years since we lived together full time," Philippa said.

"Maybe he'll get another job quickly," Chrissie pointed out, hoping the thought might help.

"Yes," said Philippa, with a smile that felt more polite than meaningful. "Perhaps."

Chrissie picked up her book and pretended to read. The truth was that after last night, she could hardly keep the smile off her face, or the flashbacks from returning at the most inopportune moments. Maybe things would work out after all. No one was perfect, she knew that for certain, and taking a risk on Nisha, on their relationship, maybe even on love, was increasingly feeling like the right thing.

She could hear Nisha a few rows back, listening politely to a monologue from Hardev about the different classifications of driving licenses, and asking the occasional question. She clearly had better concentration skills than Chrissie did this morning.

They arrived back in Birmingham late afternoon, the coach pulling up outside the school where parents were milling about.

"Daddy!" shouted Dottie. "Mummy, look, Daddy is here! I didn't know he was picking us up!"

Philippa plastered on a smile. "How lovely, darling. Come on now, get your things together."

Tired children slowly stepped off the coach, talking to their parents about croissants and the Eiffel Tower and ice-cream and their dormitories. To listen to them, you'd think that sharing a room with their classmates had been the highlight of the trip. And perhaps it was, thought Chrissie to herself. She'd been an only child, so she could see why sharing a room with others would be exciting. She dreaded to think how many smuggled sweets the children had eaten after lights out each night.

Soon it was just Chrissie and Nisha. Philippa had gone home with Paul and Dottie, and Dan had left to meet a friend at the pub. "I don't know how he has the energy," said Nisha.

"Me neither," said Chrissie, as the light faded and the streetlights began to come on.

"Do you know what I would really love to do right now?" asked Nisha, not even trying to stifle a yawn.

"Go on," said Chrissie, enjoying the quiet intimacy between them as they gathered their own bags.

"It's neither cool nor sexy." Chrissie laughed, and Nisha continued. "But I'd love to just take you to my place, we could have showers, put joggies and hoodies on, order takeout and watch TV."

Chrissie sighed. "That sounds like possibly the best idea you've ever had. Do you have enough loungewear for me?"

"Yes, although I suspect it will be too short for you."

"Well, as it's only you who'll see me, I don't think that's going to be a problem," replied Chrissie, smiling at Nisha.

"Good," said Nisha.

"I do have one condition," said Chrissie. Nisha raised her eyebrows to indicate she was listening. "There must be cuddling involved."

Nisha held out her hand. "Deal," she said, as Chrissie shook it. The warmth from Nisha's hand felt good, like the promise of something still to come. The school trip was over, but their story was only just beginning.

Again.

Chapter Forty-Three

The Vine was busy, the Christmas decorations already dripping from the ceiling. "It's a bit early for all this," said Rae, meeting Chrissie with a kiss on her cheek.

"Never too early for Christmas," replied Chrissie with a grin.

"You're on good form," said Rae, taking a seat.

"Well, yes, I guess so," Chrissie agreed.

"If I didn't know better, I'd say that something happened on that school trip." Rae had put their elbows on the table, and was giving their friend a hard stare.

"Ok," said Chrissie, blushing, "it's a fair cop."

"You and Nisha?" said Rae.

"Me and Nisha. Oh Rae, honestly, I'm so happy. I know I said I had all those rules and I couldn't break them, but I realised that you can't live life by the same strict set of rules the whole time. You have to let your life breathe – like you let your body breathe in yoga."

"Nice," said Rae, "sounds amazing. And for what it's worth, I'm really pleased for you. You deserve to be happy."

"I used to think I didn't deserve that, not after what I'd done," Chrissie told her, picking up her phone to scan the QR code and scroll through the menu.

"None of us are perfect," said Rae. "And on that note, I need to tell you about Clodagh."

"Oh yes," said Chrissie, remembering the cold look Rae's girlfriend had given her. "Is everything ok with you both?"

"Really good," Rae said, grinning. "But I think I ought to explain something. When you met her a few weeks back, no doubt you noticed she seemed a little 'off' with you."

Chrissie nodded, unsure of what was coming next.

"I asked her about it," said Rae.

"God, you're so good at just having the difficult conversation, aren't you?" said Chrissie, genuinely impressed at her young friend.

"So, it seems she's pretty friendly with Kiera, your ex."

"Ah," nodded Chrissie, a frown forming. "That would explain it. And of course it's her right not to like me."

"Well, yes," said Rae, "her right not to like you, but not her right to be gittish about it. You didn't hurt her." They steepled their fingers. "We talked about it, and Clodagh realised she'd been a bit cold and unpleasant towards you. She said she wanted to apologise."

"Oh hell, don't let her do that," said Chrissie, "that would be mortifying!"

Rae chuckled. "I thought that might be the case."

"Let's just start again next time we meet." Chrissie looked up before continuing. "Assuming there will be a next time."

"Yes, there will," said Rae. "I'm sure of it. She's threatened to turn up at my yoga class next week, which could be entertaining. She's very bendy, but she's not very co-ordinated."

Chrissie dissolved into laughter. "I really don't want to know any more about this woman!"

"It's nice to hear you laugh," said Rae. "I think this Nisha could be good for you. Maybe you'll introduce us?"

"Maybe," said Chrissie, "although it's still very early days."

"I have a good feeling about this." Rae shot Chrissie a wink. Chrissie could see why they were a hit with the bubbly-seeming Clodagh.

"But in the meantime, I need to think about my future more generally," said Chrissie.

"Oh yes?" Rae put their head to one side, the back of their mullet drooping over their shoulder.

"Yes. An opportunity's come up at the school for a graduate teacher training place. I thought I'd need to give up working there if I was going to train as a teacher, but apparently not."

Chrissie had been thrilled when she'd spotted the opportunity advertised on the noticeboard. It would of course be promoted outside the school too, but it was a chance to train to be a teacher on the job.

"I keep meaning to talk to the head about it, but if I'm honest, I'm sort of afraid of what she'll say." Chrissie bit her lip.

"Training to be a teacher?" said Rae. "What a great idea. You should so go for it."

"I'm not sure," said Chrissie. "It's been a long time since uni, and training to do something new feels really daunting."

"But you'd get to train while still working at your school,

right?" Rae pointed out. "That sounds ideal. You know the people, they know you. And it sounds like you're well respected there."

"Well, I guess so, but as a teaching assistant. Being an actual teacher is a whole different ball game. What if I'm not up to it? What if they tell me I'm not good enough to do it? I'd still have to work there after that." Chrissie fiddled with a serviette absentmindedly.

"But what if you *are* up to it? And what if it means a whole new career for you?" Rae paused to suck up some milkshake through an unfeasibly wide paper straw. "You enjoy what you do, and you like your colleagues. How many times have you told me you've been left in charge of a class? They just wouldn't do that if you weren't any good."

"Beggars can't be choosers," said Chrissie, ruefully.

"Oh shut up," said Rae. "What does Nisha think?"

Chrissie looked down. "I haven't told her. I'm most nervous about what she has to say about it, to be honest. She's been teaching for years and knows so much more about it. I don't think I could bear it if she didn't think I was up to it."

Rae put their chin on their hands and spoke slowly. "Have you thought about what *you* think of yourself? Have you considered whether *you* think you're up to it and how you might feel if you don't take this opportunity?" They straightened up and took another sip. "What you think about it all is really important. The most important thing, really."

"Ok, Yoda," said Chrissie, smiling shyly.

"Another drink?" said Rae.

"Sure."

Rae got halfway up before sitting back down. "I don't

want to alarm you," they said, "but there's a bloke over there staring right at you. Do you know him?"

Chrissie's heart sank as she looked across to see the man with long white hair.

Lucian. He looked even more unkempt than he had done before.

Chapter Forty-Four

ONE YEAR EARLIER

C hrissie was hovering in the shrubbery near a layby. Her feet hurt because she'd walked for what felt like miles to reach the road. She felt strangely untethered, having left Lucian and the group behind. She felt afraid.

For the last nine months she had done everything Lucian had said, given him money, stayed in the middle of nowhere, eaten at particular times of the day. More recently the food had become more scarce – part of their spiritual test, he said. But something inside Chrissie was calling to her. There was something wrong with this. It had nagged at her before, but now she knew she needed to get away from him.

That day, he'd made a careless mistake. He'd put down his phone and walked away – a phone he denied even owning, as he'd told them all that he, like they, had abandoned his connection to the outside world, to modern technology, to western medicine. Chrissie had spotted it, and, blood thundering in her ears, she'd managed to open it, establish where she was, and get a message to Kiera.

Then she ran.

Now hiding as well as she could among the undergrowth and litter, she hoped against hope that Kiera would find it in her heart to rescue her. But would hope be enough? Deep down, she didn't believe Kiera would come.

When the familiar car pulled up, she could hardly believe it.

Chrissie couldn't speak to start with, and was shocked when she saw her own reflection in the wing mirror. She didn't recognise the grey, thin face in front of her, the long, lank, tangled hair. She knew in that moment she had done the right thing by running. But she had no idea what she was going to do next.

Chapter Forty-Five

C hrissie stood abruptly, and before she had even thought it through, walked over to Lucian. He seemed startled at her approach. But it was time to take control. She couldn't spend the rest of her life afraid of him.

She heard Rae's chair legs drag across the floor, and knew they were just a few steps behind. That gave her confidence.

"You need to leave me alone," said Chrissie, her voice low and strong.

"I'm just having a cup of tea in a café," Lucian replied with a smile. "No law against that."

"No, you're following me. You came to my house and now you come here and stare at me. No more. You need to leave and never come back," Chrissie told him. She could feel her voice wobbling, but drew strength from Rae, who was now standing next to her.

"I think you wanted me to find you," said Lucian. "You always had such potential. I think you want to get back into the process."

"No," said Chrissie, her voice closer to a shout. "Leave me alone. If I ever see you near me again, I will call the police." She took a step forward. "And if you say one more word to me I will scream."

Lucian opened his mouth.

"Not one more word, you horrible little man," said Chrissie.

"You heard her," said Rae, their arms folded.

Lucian pursed his lips and glared at Chrissie. Her breathing quickened as she prepared herself for what he was going to do or say next. But she knew that whatever happened, she had to believe in herself.

Lucian looked around himself, and then stood, bringing himself close enough that Chrissie could smell the remnants of the lavender incense he loved so much. He sniffed. "The tea in here is rubbish anyway."

He turned tail and walked out.

Chrissie was breathing hard as she watched him leave. Rae held out their hand and grasped Chrissie's.

"You ok?" they asked gently.

"Yes," said Chrissie. "Yes, I am." She felt a smile form on her face. "I think perhaps I need a stiff drink, but apart from that, I'm actually good." She walked back to their table. "I've never stood up to him before," she continued. "I was so scared, but I knew I had to face him, to tell him no, not this time and not ever again. He doesn't have control over me anymore."

"Bravo!" said Rae, their face transformed by a broad smile. "I'm getting us some Prosecco to celebrate."

Chrissie grinned. She felt shaky after the confrontation, but elated at the strength and power she felt. It was as though the last strings that had bound her to that man, to that group, to that time, had been severed.

She picked up her phone, and before she knew what she was doing, she was texting Nisha.

Chapter Forty-Six

"I see you've cracked open the good stuff," said Nisha, as she walked into the Vine.

"You came to see me?" said Chrissie, surprised to see the short figure dressed in football kit approaching.

"After hearing about such a dramatic event? I could hardly not! Besides, I'd just finished footy practice, so I can order some chips to replenish my athletic physique." Nisha patted her rounded stomach as she spoke.

Chrissie smiled. "Come here." She stood to embrace Nisha.

"I'm all muddy," warned Nisha.

"I don't care!" The couple hugged and Nisha kissed Chrissie on the cheek.

"Well done," said Nisha. "Mind if I join you? You must be Rae, I've heard how fabulous a friend you are to Chrissie." She held out her hand and Rae shook it.

"And it's wonderful to meet you, having heard about you for the last few weeks," said Rae.

"All good things, I'm sure," said Nisha with a wink.

"Well," replied Rae, "I'm not going to lie, there was a bit of angst, but lately it's definitely been good."

"I'll take that," said Nisha, waggling her eyebrows and throwing an arm around Chrissie's shoulders. "Right, I'm ordering chips. Anyone else want anything?"

"Oooh," said Chrissie, "sweet potato fries for me. It seems only fair."

"You know how to live." Nisha smiled at her before heading to the bar.

"She seems lovely," said Rae.

"I know," agreed Chrissie, grinning a stupid grin.

"Oh my God, hearts have practically popped up in your eyes. You totally love her!" exclaimed Rae, eagerly pouring out more Prosecco.

"Shhhhhhhh," said Chrissie, causing Nisha to turn around and look at them. "Don't say that!"

"I don't need to," said Rae, "your face says it all."

Chrissie laughed. Perhaps it did. And perhaps she needed to worry less about it.

An hour later they had eaten their fill of chips of both varieties, and were onto their second bottle of Prosecco. "I am going to regret this at the early morning yoga class," said Rae, slurring the words.

"I don't think I've ever seen you drunk," observed Chrissie, feeling the effects herself.

"No," said Rae, "I don't tend to drink much. Not sure what happened today."

"I'll tell you what happened," said Nisha, "Chrissie faced down the evil cult leader and told him where to stick it. And I, for one, am here for it." She raised her glass. "To Chrissie being badass."

Rae raised their glass and repeated the words.

"I feel like I'm missing a party," came a voice from a few metres away.

"Clodagh," said Rae, beaming their own smile of love – or possibly lust.

"Babe, you're totally pissed, I love it. You've never drunk texted me before, so I had to see this for myself," said Clodagh, taking in the others at the table before carefully sitting down. She paused, then politely put out her hand to Chrissie. "I don't think we got a proper chance to meet last time. I'm Clodagh. Rae's paramour."

Chrissie breathed out in relief. "Nice to meet you. I'm Chrissie." Clodagh nodded, smiled and was then introduced to Nisha by Rae.

"Now, I think it needs saying," said Clodagh, "but we're going to need more Prosecco if I'm to add any value to this little gathering. I'll be right back," she added, strolling over to the bar.

"You ok?" Rae asked. Chrissie was impressed they'd remembered the awkwardness from earlier, given how drunk they appeared to be.

"Yes, of course," said Chrissie. "Are *you* ok? It would seem you've been drunk texting your 'paramour'!" They laughed, clinked their glasses, and waited for Clodagh to return.

Later that evening, Nisha and Chrissie walked back to Chrissie's place arm in arm. "That was fun," said Nisha.

"It really was," agreed Chrissie. "It was like being on a sort of double date."

"How very rom com," said Nisha, deadpan.

"Do you mind that people know we're together?" asked Chrissie, emboldened by the bubbly.

"Do I mind?" said Nisha, pausing by a traffic light. "I bloody love it. I wish I could tell everyone that I am with

Chrissie Anderson," she added, her voice rising in volume with every word.

Chrissie giggled. "Shhh."

"Well, what about you? Do you mind people know we're together?" asked Nisha, who had begun to walk forward again.

"It depends," said Chrissie.

"On what?"

"Well, it depends on whether this is just sex for you, whether it's a fling and soon you'll leave and find someone else – someone better. Or whether it's a meaningful thing, a relationship. Whether you might want to be my girlfriend, one day, not now, obviously," said Chrissie, aware that she was beginning to ramble.

"Whoa," said Nisha, stopping once again on the pathway. "Hang on there. Do you really think this is just sex? Is that what it is for you?"

"No, of course not. It's just, well, I don't know what the next step looks like for you. We never got past this point last time," said Chrissie.

Nisha looked thoughtful for a moment. "Yes, I guess that makes sense. Ok," she said, "let's get into the warm of your place and I will explain to you exactly what this is, at least from my perspective."

Chapter Forty-Seven

Nisha sat on Chrissie's bed fresh from the shower, a towel wrapped around her. "Thanks for this," she said. "I was far too muddy for public consumption. Well, for your consumption."

Chrissie giggled. "Ok, come on then, explain 'what we are'." She'd changed into her pyjamas while Nisha had been showering, and was admiring her companion's bare shoulders.

"Well, I mean, I don't have all the answers. You're just as much a part of this as I am. But I can tell you that for me, this means something," said Nisha, a drop of water falling from her tousled hair onto her chest. Chrissie put out a finger to gently wipe it away. "You mean a lot to me. And I wouldn't be doing any of this if I didn't think we had some kind of meaningful future."

"Really?" said Chrissie, shocked by how precisely Nisha was saying exactly the words she wanted to hear. She wondered how far she should question this. But then, she'd questioned being with Nisha so much, for so long, perhaps it was time to stop.

"Really," replied Nisha. "We're too old to play around. You are funny and kind and thoughtful and slightly flighty, but I love you for it."

"You what?" said Chrissie in a whisper.

Nisha's face reddened. Then she looked directly at Chrissie and took her hand. "I love you, Chrissie."

Chrissie could feel tears begin to well up, and swallowed hard. "You love me," she repeated.

"Yes," agreed Nisha. "And you really shouldn't leave a girl hanging." She laughed nervously.

"Oh my," said Chrissie. "I mean, I'm in love with you. I think I always was. But the moment you walked into that classroom with your dimple and your beautiful eyes, the day you made me run around in the mud and the rain. I knew I loved you. I hated that I loved you, but I did." Chrissie stroked Nisha's hair and cupped her cheek. "But now, I love that I love you too."

Nisha smiled, and leaned in to kiss Chrissie on the lips. Chrissie closed her eyes. "It suddenly feels so easy," she said, as she pulled away.

"Maybe that's the Prosecco talking," said Nisha, "or maybe we've been getting in our own way until now."

"It's not just the Prosecco," said Chrissie, undoing Nisha's towel and straddling her lap. "But I know for sure I've been getting in my own way until today."

Nisha leaned back, her hands behind her on the bed. "Well, cheers to us growing up!"

Chrissie kissed her neck and ran her hand down her cleavage. "Yes, here's to that."

Chapter Forty-Eight

Chrissie tried to remember her pranayama breathing as she sat outside Mrs Hemingway's office, waiting to be called in. As a child, she'd always assumed that it was only the pupils that got nervous while waiting to be summoned. The older she got, the more she realised that no one really ever lets go of their inner child's insecurities.

The door opened. "Miss Anderson," said Mrs Hemingway. "Come in and take a seat."

The head teacher's office smelled of pencil shavings and coffee, and had a painting of Birmingham's Victoria Square lit up by the city's Christmas market on the wall.

"It'll be opening back up again soon," said Chrissie, gesturing to the painting.

"Yes, I can't wait," replied Mrs Hemingway, showing uncharacteristic excitement. "I know not everyone cares for it, but I make sure I go several times over the season. It really brightens up some of the darker weeks of the year."

"It does," agreed Chrissie, making a mental note to make sure to go there with Nisha.

Mrs Hemingway sat behind her desk. "I know you asked to see me," she said, "but before that, I wanted to congratulate you on the fantastic school trip to Paris."

"Oh," said Chrissie, taken by surprise. "Thank you."

"I've heard rave reviews both from the children and their parents." Mrs Hemingway straightened a pencil on her desk. "As you know, I did have my doubts, but the fact that you and Ms Rajan managed to pull it off, along with Mr Harvey, is really something to celebrate."

"Well, thank you," said Chrissie again. "And I must mention Dottie's mum, Philippa. She was the person who helped us secure the funding, and she was a brilliant support on the trip itself."

"Yes," said Mrs Hemingway, "I've spoken to her too. She is something of a dynamic presence on our PTA. But, Miss Anderson, if you don't mind me saying, without your enthusiasm and confidence in the children, this would never have happened." She looked Chrissie in the eye. "Well done."

Chrissie didn't know what to say. She hadn't expected this, especially since Mrs Hemingway wasn't known for giving unqualified praise.

"Now," continued the head teacher. "I'm here to listen to what you have to say. How can I help you?"

Chrissie gathered her thoughts, momentarily discombobulated by the unexpected direction the conversation had taken. She put her hands together and began. "I've seen that you're advertising for someone to do a graduate teacher training placement next year. I was thinking about applying for it."

She took a deep breath in and waited.

Mrs Hemingway beamed. "Yes, of course. I assumed

you would, to be honest. I'd be delighted to see your application."

"Great, well," said Chrissie, rising from her seat. "I'll definitely get that to you."

"Lovely," said Mrs Hemingway. "The deadline is the end of the week, so crack on."

Chrissie spent the rest of the day planning out in her head how she would write her application, imagining what it would be like to return the next academic year as a trainee teacher.

In yoga later that evening, she felt a strength and calmness she hadn't experienced for a long time. She rested in downward dog, breathing in rhythm with the rest of the class, and emptied her mind. She allowed herself to be guided by Rae's voice, moving her limbs in sequence, finding her flow. Flow was a word Rae used a lot in classes, and today it felt more apt than ever before.

"You look happy," said Rae, while they and Chrissie tidied up after the class.

"I am," agreed Chrissie. "I sort of feel like I've moved into a new chapter of my life. I have a sense of who I am now, what I'm doing, and where I'm going."

"That is really awesome," said Rae. "I'm so pleased. I knew I liked Nisha."

"It's not just Nisha," said Chrissie, thoughtfully. "In many ways, I think had we met a few months earlier, it wouldn't have worked at all. I think that in truth, part of it is about time. But you've played a role in all this too."

"Me?" said Rae, whipping their head round from the cupboard they were putting yoga blocks into.

"Yes," said Chrissie. "You've been there for me through everything, right from when I barely knew who I was or what I stood for anymore. You've been the one who's been reassuring, asked me questions, pushed me to push myself, and all in the spirit of love and friendship."

"Aw, mate," said Rae, with a half-smile, "that's such a lovely thing to say." They stood and turned towards Chrissie. "Permission to hug?"

"Granted!" replied Chrissie with a laugh. The friends embraced. "But it's all true. Thank you, I really appreciate you and everything you've done for me."

Rae pulled away. "It's not a one-way street, Chrissie. You've been there for me, too. Always a smiling face in my classes, always helping set up and pack away, always listening to my troubles. I feel lucky to have such a great friend."

Chrissie felt warm inside and out, confident that this was the beginning of the best time of her life.

Chapter Forty-Nine

The frost made Kings Heath Park look sparkly, with trees emerging glistening through the mist. Chrissie was in her favourite baggy yellow woolly hat and her pink wellies, and Nisha was wearing a purple beanie and her walking boots. Their gloved hands were clasped together as they strolled.

"Look," said Chrissie, "the pond is iced over in places. The moorhens are walking along the surface."

Nisha laughed. "They look so funny. I love that you notice things like that."

"What can I say, I'm observant," said Chrissie, squeezing Nisha's hand. "I noticed you, after all."

"I think you'll find I'm hard to miss," replied Nisha, the hot air emerging from her mouth as mist.

"You may be right," said Chrissie, grinning. "Especially that day you were playing football over there in the pouring rain."

"Ha, yes, that was a great day," said Nisha, taking her hand out of Chrissie's in order to put her arm around her girlfriend's shoulders. "And not least because you kissed me."

"Oh God, yes. I had a bit of a moment that day," said Chrissie.

"Well, my love, I'm glad you did."

"That's a nice thing to say," said Chrissie, feeling warm. "And talking of moments, I need to tell you that I've decided to apply for that teacher training place that Ernest's been advertising." She clenched her teeth, waiting for Nisha's response. "I got all nervous the other day when I went to talk to her about it."

"Well I hope you didn't kiss her," jested Nisha. "But seriously, that's awesome. You will be an incredible teacher."

"Do you really think so?" asked Chrissie.

"I do," said Nisha. "I've learnt from you since we've been working together. And while I'd miss having you in my classroom next year, it would be amazing to see you teaching your own class."

"Thank you!" exclaimed Chrissie, relieved to have the support of her girlfriend.

Nisha's phone started to vibrate in her coat pocket. They were so close, Chrissie could feel it. Nisha took the phone out and looked at it, frowning. "I should take this," she said. "Why don't you order us teas in the café over there and I'll join you in a sec."

"Sure," said Chrissie, wondering who was calling Nisha on a Saturday morning in December.

Chrissie sat at a formica-covered table with two steaming cups of tea. The windows of the café had begun to cloud, the heat of the people inside battling with the cold outside. She'd bought a couple of flapjacks too, to keep them going. It had been fifteen minutes, but she wasn't concerned. Nisha had had a whole life before they'd reunited, and had many friends, and of course family.

Finally, Nisha came in. Chrissie couldn't place the expression on her face. She looked like she was frowning, but in thought, perhaps, rather than unhappiness.

"You ok?" asked Chrissie.

"Yeah, sure, just a friend asking a favour," said Nisha, sitting down. "Thanks for the tea. I needed it. I think I've lost the sensation in my toes."

Chrissie gave Nisha an appraising look, but decided to leave it. It was Nisha's stuff, not Chrissie's.

"Yeah, I know what you mean. I got us a sweet treat to help encourage the blood flow," said Chrissie.

Nisha looked down at her phone without replying. She seemed to have forgotten their earlier conversation about teacher training.

"I was thinking we should do the Christmas market sometime this week," said Chrissie, trying to bring Nisha out of her funk.

"Yeah, why not," Nisha replied, looking up briefly, before poking her flapjack with her index finger.

"What's up?" asked Chrissie, finally, not sure she could pretend any longer that Nisha's demeanour hadn't completely changed.

"Sorry," said Nisha. "I just wasn't expecting that call."

"I can tell that," said Chrissie, "but what was it? If it's ok to ask, that is. I don't want to pry, but you look a bit shell-shocked."

"I guess I am." Nisha took a sip of her tea. "It was Jake."

Chrissie's eyebrows almost leapt off her head. "Jake. Your ex?" Her mind was racing, not so much because he'd called, more because of Nisha's complete change in mood.

"Yes," Nisha replied.

"I didn't think you were in touch with him," said Chrissie.

"I wasn't, you're right. But recently, since you and me happened, I felt I owed him a bit of an apology. I ran out on him – as you know, a bit of a habit of mine," said Nisha.

"You told him you were sorry you left him?" said Chrissie, feeling fingers of fear begin to creep into her brain.

"Sort of," said Nisha. Then she looked up and saw Chrissie's concerned face. "No," she added, "not like that. Our split was a joint decision. I wasn't apologising for that."

"Ok, so tell me what's happened now," said Chrissie, trying to hang on to her breath, her balance, her centre.

"I emailed him a few weeks ago to say I was sorry I'd left London without sorting things out properly. That was wrong of me. The relationship was over, but I didn't handle the difficult stuff well, and, as you know, I ran to Birmingham." Nisha took a small bite of her flapjack, clearly still mulling something over.

"And he called you?" asked Chrissie, keen to understand what was happening here.

"Yes, he did. And given I was the one who'd emailed him, when I saw his name on the phone, I knew I had to answer. When I first left London, I ignored his calls, and eventually he just gave up calling," said Nisha. "He was calling to say thanks for apologising."

"Well, I guess that's good," said Chrissie, trying to be adult and reasonable and not dissolve into a pool of jealousy.

"Yes, I think so," Nisha agreed. "But he also had something else to say. He was letting me know that the head teacher at the school I used to teach at with him has left unexpectedly, and they're looking for someone to act as head for the next twelve months. Given the school is in a challenging area, with children with all sorts of complex needs, they want someone who's already familiar with it. He's deputy at the moment, and he's been asked to approach me by the Chair of the Board of Governors, to see if I'd be willing to act as head teacher from January."

Chapter Fifty

C hrissie's phone buzzed by the side of her bed. It was ten on a Sunday morning. Normally she would have gone to yoga, but after yesterday's revelation from Nisha, she'd prioritised sleep in the hope things would feel better today.

She opened her eyes. Things did not feel better. The conversation the previous day had jarred with everything she had begun to assume about their relationship. Nisha was contemplating moving back to London for a year. It was a professional opportunity that might be too good to miss. Chrissie's eyes roamed the artexed ceiling above her. Nisha had suggested she could go with her. It didn't feel right, somehow, following her girlfriend back to her old life.

Chrissie didn't think Nisha was getting back together with Jake, but the thought of her returning to that school felt wrong. And Chrissie had a life here in Birmingham, one she had fought hard to build. And it wasn't just that. She was so close to taking her own steps towards becoming a qualified teacher.

"You could do that in London, at my school," said Nisha, grabbing Chrissie's hand across the table in the café when she had raised the point.

"And leave everything I've created for myself here?" said Chrissie. "I don't know whether I can. And you don't even know if there will be a training position at the school in London."

"I'd be head, though," said Nisha, her eyes shining. "I could make it happen."

"No," said Chrissie, firmly. "Absolutely not. I am not being given a free pass because my girlfriend's the head teacher. I won't do that." She pressed her mouth together in a straight line.

"Yes, sorry," agreed Nisha, immediately apologetic. "I knew that sounded wrong the moment it came out of my mouth. No, of course I wouldn't do that." She sighed. "But there could be an opportunity at another school nearby."

"But the thing is," said Chrissie, "I need to own my own space here, and I need to do the right things for me. If I chase you to London for this opportunity, where would you go next? Back to Birmingham after that year? What if they gave you the job permanently? I can't hang onto your coat tails." Her stomach churned as she said words she knew might change their relationship irretrievably, but at the same time, she knew it was true: she had to hang onto herself and what she needed.

"I get it," said Nisha. "But can't you see this is a massive opportunity for me?"

"I absolutely can," said Chrissie. "But at the same time, I can also see how it impacts on us in ways I'm not totally sure about." She balled her fists in her lap. "If you want to take the job, you should totally do it," she continued. "I couldn't forgive myself for holding you back. But I'm not sure I can follow you there."

Nisha's eyes widened in fear. "But what do you mean? That this would be all over? That this would be a distance relationship?"

"Nisha," said Chrissie, "I don't know what I mean. I'm just telling you how I feel as I sit here right now in front of you. I don't want to end this, absolutely not. I love you. But I also know I need to make sure I don't destroy the fragile life I've built for myself here in Kings Heath."

"Of course," Nisha replied, quietly. Her eyes were beginning to look red, and Chrissie worried she might cry, something Nisha very rarely did. "You're right, of course you are. You need to focus on what you need. I'm sorry, I've sort of landed this on you with no warning. I feel a bit taken aback by it myself. But know this," she said, laying her hand on Chrissie's, "I love you too. I am sure we can work this out."

Chrissie smiled at her, but the smile didn't touch her eyes. She wasn't convinced they would be able to work it out.

"I feel like the world is getting in our way, now," said Chrissie. And as she rolled out of bed the next morning, she picked up her phone and yawned. The day felt drained of colour.

She made herself a peach iced tea to try and inject some vibrancy into the morning. She thought back to Nisha's suggestion that they could try and have a distance relationship – take it in turns to travel to see each other every weekend. It was a possibility, she supposed. But it wasn't one that filled Chrissie with hope, even though it would only be for a year. In truth, she knew how good Nisha was at her job, and felt sure the twelve-month contract would be extended. And who was Chrissie to hold her back and tell her she needed to come back to her in Birmingham?

She opened her phone to find a text message from Nisha, wishing her a good morning with a kissing emoji. Chrissie groaned. They'd gone their separate ways the day before, sleeping in their respective beds for the first time in a few weeks. It felt like a sign. It was time to get the journal out and try to work things through in her own mind before she did anything else.

Chapter Fifty-One

B its of tinsel were beginning to appear around the
school, much to the children's delight. It brightened up
an otherwise grey and rainy Monday morning. Dottie,
Francis and Hardev and their classmates were working hard
on their maths, while Nisha and Chrissie looked over the
syllabus to see what they still needed to cover by the time the
Christmas holidays rolled in.

"I think we've done pretty well so far this term," said
Nisha. "They can be a bit of a handful, but they're getting
on well."

"Yeah," agreed Chrissie, following Nisha's finger down
the educational 'to-do' list. "They've really taken to you,
which I think helps hugely."

Nisha smiled. "Thanks," she said. But sadness swiftly
filled the gap between them. This was a class that might
need a new teacher again in a couple of months. "I could
turn the job offer down," she whispered.

"We can't talk about this here," said Chrissie, her voice
low, knowing that she would never ask Nisha to turn down

the opportunity of a lifetime. She couldn't be that selfish. Never again.

"Ah," came a decisive voice from the classroom door. "Miss Anderson, if I might have a quick word, please?"

Mrs Hemingway was looming over the class, all the children having turned around to look at her, their eyes wide. "Good morning, Mrs He-ming-way," they chanted, as they'd been taught to in reception whenever a teacher visited the class.

"And good morning to you all, class," replied Mrs Hemingway, with her most encouraging smile. The children beamed. She might be a bit of a mystery to the staff team, but the children adored her.

"Excuse me a moment," said Chrissie to the class. "I'll be right back." She couldn't push down the increase in her heart rate. Mrs Hemingway had never pulled her out of class like this before, and she sensed it heralded something very good, or alternatively, something very bad. She scanned through her memories of the last couple of weeks at school and tried to recall anything she might have done to merit a telling off. Beyond calling Hardev a 'wally', which she was fully prepared to defend – mainly because he was being one at the time – she couldn't think of anything. But her nerves were very much apparent as Mrs Hemingway shut the classroom door behind them and they stood together in the hallway.

"Thank you, Miss Anderson, so sorry to disturb you. Now, I'll get right to business. I want to offer you a teacher training post here, starting in September next year," said Mrs Hemingway, all business.

Chrissie gulped. "Really?"

"You seem surprised. You really shouldn't be," said the head teacher, patting Chrissie on the shoulder like she was one of the children. "You've been an asset to this school ever since you started, and I have absolutely no doubt you will be an exceptional teacher."

"Thank you," said Chrissie, aware that while this improved her professional life no end, it added another layer of complication to her personal situation.

"It would of course mean hard work next year – teaching in school and also studying at college for part of the time. Assignments, and the like," Mrs Hemingway told her. "But I don't doubt for a moment that you are up to that."

"I hope so," said Chrissie, slightly breathless in the moment.

"So," said the head teacher, "will you accept?"

"Of course!" replied Chrissie, knowing she had even more to think about now than she'd had just a few minutes earlier.

"You and Ms Rajan make quite the team," said Mrs Hemingway, with a wink. "I'm sure she'll prove very supportive to you next year, as you teach side by side."

"Yes," agreed Chrissie. Nisha obviously hadn't told Mrs Hemingway about the likelihood of her imminent departure. And it wasn't Chrissie's news to share.

Chrissie returned to the classroom, Nisha's eyes looking quizzically over at hers. She couldn't say anything know, though.

"I'll tell you later," she mouthed, wondering how Nisha would take the news.

Chapter Fifty-Two

Chrissie bubbled inside with excitement. In spite of everything that was going on with Nisha, she knew this was a good thing, and the right thing for her. She knew now that she definitely couldn't move to London. This was her own opportunity, and she needed to take it.

She sat down with Dan and Nisha, and they opened their respective packed lunch boxes.

"So," said Dan, "I hear that training position was announced today. Do you have anything to tell us?"

Nisha looked at Chrissie immediately, and she could feel herself turning bright red. "I knew it!" said Nisha. "The minute Mrs H came to get you, I knew that was what she was telling you. You got it!" She squeezed Chrissie's hand.

"I got it," confirmed Chrissie, a wide grin forming on her face.

"Proud of you," said Nisha, "that really is the best news." There was an odd expression on Nisha's face that Chrissie assumed had everything to do with the fact that the universe seeming to be pulling them apart.

"Me too," said Dan, "although I must confess, I helped with some of the selection discussions, so I knew."

"You git," said Chrissie, "you should have said!"

"I was sworn to secrecy by she who must be obeyed," said Dan, glancing dramatically over his shoulder.

"Ah yes, the ever-present Mrs H," said Nisha. And as if by magic, the woman herself swept into the room.

"Good afternoon, everybody," said the head teacher, and the room fell into a sudden silence, save for one or two rustling crisp packets. She had the same effect on the staff as she did on the pupils. "I'm afraid I have news to share that may have an impact on the rest of your working week." She paused, as if to build the tension. "I have had the call."

They all knew what that meant. Chrissie could hear murmurs of "Ofsted" from the mouths of her colleagues, all aware that the rest of their week had been bulldozed by government inspectors.

"That means," said Mrs Hemingway, raising her voice over the increased noise, "that we have forty-eight hours before they arrive on Wednesday afternoon. We knew we were due an inspection, so now we know it's happening this week. I know there will be things that heads of departments will need to start getting together, and no doubt meetings to call, but before we get on with this, I have something important to say." She paused, and the silence seemed to deepen. The room was now even fuller, as word had got round the school.

Mrs Hemingway took a breath. "You are an incredible group of teachers and teaching assistants. You teach at one of the most diverse schools in the city, and you prepare hundreds of children for the outside world every day. I have every faith in you. So, yes," she said, "do your preparation, have those meetings, but know that you are the best team I have had the pleasure to work with, and you will do an amazing job."

And with that, she left the room.

"Wow," said Dan. "I don't know whether to feel terrified of the inspectors, pleased Mrs H loves us all so much, or frightened of letting her down."

"Yes," said Nisha, "it's an odd mix of emotions."

Chrissie nodded. She felt it too.

"Right," Nisha continued. "Let's get our heads together after work. We need to bring together all the paperwork for our section of the school."

Chrissie and Dan nodded, resigned to their fate. It was going to be a long day. Nisha's phone lit up, and she looked down. She frowned as she scanned her screen, then grimaced as she tapped out a response.

Chapter Fifty-Three

"Are we all happy?" asked Nisha, looking around the room at the six or seven colleagues she was coordinating as they prepared for the inspection.

"Ecstatic," replied Dan, rolling his eyes.

"Ok, smart-arse," said Nisha, "perhaps not happy, but do we all know what we're doing?"

"We do," said Dan, and the others nodded. Chrissie sat quietly at the back of the room. Most of the other teaching assistants had already gone home.

Soon it was just Chrissie and Nisha left in the room, with empty coffee mugs and three empty biscuit packets strewn across the desks.

"Honestly," said Nisha, "they're worse than the kids for not clearing up after themselves." She looked up at Chrissie as she gathered up the rubbish. "Thanks for staying. You know you didn't have to."

"I know," said Chrissie, "but I wanted to support you. And besides, I need to get used to this stuff."

"Yes," agreed Nisha, raising her eyebrows. "Yes, you're

right, you do. Congrats, Chris. Your news has been swept up into all this, but I want you to know how proud I am of you." She walked over to Chrissie, who was standing with her back to a phonics display board. She put her arms around her and held her. Chrissie brought her arms up to Nisha's back and allowed her head to fall on Nisha's shoulder. It felt so good to be together, sharing this moment in this way. But it only made it more painful, knowing their days were probably numbered.

Chrissie brought her lips to the smooth skin on Nisha's neck and planted a soft kiss. "Thank you. Whatever happens now, I'll never regret this," said Chrissie.

Nisha put her finger to Chrissie's chin and brought her face up. "Nor will I," she said. "Do you want to stay at mine tonight?"

Chrissie smiled, a sadness in her heart. "I'm not sure I can," she said. "I'm not angry, I'm just trying to sort things out in my head. You wanted to stop running away from things, and I can see you've made that change in facing Jake, going back to your new school, taking this amazing opportunity. And I want to be happy for you. I really do. But right now, I need some time to process that. I hope you understand."

Nisha frowned. "I'm sorry. Yes, you must take all the time to yourself you need. I can see I've made things hard for you and I feel bad about that. How about we get through Ofsted and then regroup on Friday? We can work everything out then."

"Ms Rajan," said Mrs Hemingway, once again looming in the doorway. The two women leapt apart, Chrissie pretending to be pinning up work that had been displayed since September and Nisha collecting mugs. "I wonder if you might have a moment to discuss your email?" the head teacher asked, a smile playing on her lips.

"Certainly," said Nisha, more formally than she would normally talk even to Mrs Hemingway. She was obviously trying to make up for being caught in an embrace with a colleague in the workplace. Chrissie giggled quietly, in spite of herself.

Alone in the classroom, Chrissie had a sinking feeling. She didn't know exactly what they were talking about, but realistically, it had to be about Nisha's new job in London. Nisha would have emailed the head teacher to let her know. Chrissie looked up at the display she'd been pretending to amend, displaying all the different colours of autumn leaves. She was reminded of something her father once told her – that some friends were for a reason and some for a season. Perhaps she and Nisha had only ever been passing leaves in the breeze. They gave each other what they needed at the time, then moved onto their own paths, moving in opposite directions.

Chrissie shook her head to try and rid herself of the vision of her and Nisha as leaves, floating away from one another.

Chapter Fifty-Four

C hrissie's doorbell went. It was past nine pm and she didn't think it would be Nisha – they'd agreed to give each other a bit of space until the end of the week.

She went to the door to find Philippa standing there, smartly dressed as usual, holding two carrier bags of what smelt suspiciously like curry.

"You may already have eaten, but Dottie told me you got the call from Ofsted, so I thought you might need some additional sustenance," said Philippa.

"How does that girl find out everything that happens in the school?" asked Chrissie with a laugh.

"Try living with her," replied Philippa, deadpan.

"I have eaten," said Chrissie, "but I think I may have a separate stomach for naan bread and paneer, so come on in."

Philippa grinned. "I also wanted to say well done on the training place you secured – thanks for texting to let me know."

"Ah, you're welcome," said Chrissie, showing Philippa

into the kitchen and getting out plates and cutlery. "It was partly you that encouraged me to apply."

"Well, you deserve it," said Philippa. "But may I say, you look exhausted. Was it a long one?"

"It really was," said Chrissie. "Wait, where is Dottie?"

"At home with her father," replied Philippa, her mouth pursing. "He's in the house all the time now."

"Oh yes, of course," said Chrissie. "He's not found another job yet, then?"

"No," said Philippa with a sigh. "He's talking about taking early retirement and working on his golf handicap."

Chrissie wasn't sure why this was such bad news, but if the look on her face was anything to go by, then for Philippa, it clearly was.

"But enough about him. How about you? Are you getting on ok?" asked Philippa, clearly keen not to talk too much about her own domestic situation.

"Yeah, ok, I guess," said Chrissie with a shrug.

The friends sat down at the small kitchen table. "Everything ok with Nisha?"

Philippa was incapable of holding back, and Chrissie knew she had to tell her something. But she couldn't tell her the truth, not with Nisha being Dottie's class teacher. It wouldn't be fair.

"Things are a bit tricky, to be honest," said Chrissie. "I can't go into it in detail. It wouldn't be fair," she added, pulling apart the naan bread so they could both have some. "It's like our lives continue to pull us in different directions. I just wonder whether it's really meant to be something that lasts."

"Oh," said Philippa, her face falling. She looked genuinely upset. "But you seem so good together."

"Oh, we are," Chrissie agreed, through a mouthful of

bhuna. "But what's the line in that John Lennon song? Life is what happens to you while you're busy making other plans? It's sort of like that. I don't want to hold her back."

"I don't think you could," said Philippa. "I'm not going to pry, it's your business. But have faith. I feel like the two of you are supposed to be together. Didn't you say you were a thing back when you were in your teens?"

"Yes," replied Chrissie, with a smile. "It was a summer of hope and naivety and dreams and for a few weeks, it was perfect. Then we went our separate ways and didn't see each other for twenty years."

"It sounds wonderful," said Philippa, looking wistfully up and over Chrissie's head, as if remembering something from her own past. "I didn't do anything nearly as interesting when I was in my teens. It makes me wish I had." She looked back at Chrissie, her cheeks pink.

"It's never too late, you know," said Chrissie. "I know that to be a hard, cold fact."

"Hmm," said Philippa. "Yes, perhaps. But keep your hope and naivety, Chrissie, it suits you. Things may work out still."

"We'll see. But before that," said Chrissie, wiping a blob of sauce from her plate with her naan, "we need to get through this wretched inspection."

"Yes, although I feel like between you, Dan, Nisha and Mrs Hemingway, you will absolutely smash it."

"Is that a legal term?" asked Chrissie.

"Of course," replied Philippa, elegantly wiping the corner of her mouth with a piece of kitchen roll. "We always promise ourselves that the night before a big case. And we always order in curry."

"Well, thank you for making me part of your tradition," said Chrissie, touched that Philippa had thought of her.

Chapter Fifty-Five

The next day there was a fevered energy to the school. There were only twenty-four hours until the inspectors were due to descend, and there was a lot to do. Chrissie found herself busy replacing all the tired displays from one of the hallways, trying to make the learning environment look as 'vibrant' as an Ofsted inspector could dream of.

"What is that supposed to be?" asked Dan as he hurried past her.

"Rude," called Chrissie, "you can clearly see that it's a crocodile. It's a new display on books the children have loved this year."

"Oh yes, of course," said Dan, papers clutched to his front. "Sorry, thought it was a green turd for a moment!" and with that, he disappeared around the corner.

"Charming," said Chrissie, with a laugh, grateful for her colleagues and their support, however differently they all showed it.

"Nice," said Nisha, emerging into the corridor from the classroom for a moment. "An avocado, I assume?"

"Very droll," replied Chrissie, rolling her eyes.

"Sorry," said Nisha, "I heard Dan and I couldn't resist. Although now all the children have heard him say the word 'turd', so I have some serious reverse-engineering to do."

"Tell them he was saying 'curd'," said Chrissie, "like Little Miss Muffet and her curds and whey."

"How very Victorian," said Nisha. "But I might well try that. Although I feel that, with Hardev and Dottie in the room, that genius plan won't survive for long."

"True. Now, once I have the teeth on this thing, it will all become clear," said Chrissie.

"It will." Nisha smiled, then pulled out her phone from her pocket, before frowning at it again.

"All ok?" asked Chrissie, hardly bearing to know the answer. She knew it would be Jake, and she knew it would be about London.

"Yep," said Nisha, plastering on a smile and disappearing back into the classroom.

Everyone was anxious about the arrival of the inspection team the next day, but Chrissie felt more worried about the outcome of the conversation she and Nisha had planned for Friday night, once the inspectors had gone. It was clear that Nisha was still very distracted, which did not bode well.

At half past eight that night they left the school, after a final staff meeting with Mrs Hemingway at the helm. Even she had seemed slightly frazzled, a strand of her hair uncharacteristically freeing itself from her hair band.

"Do you want a quick glass of wine at the Vine?" asked Chrissie, as she and Nisha crossed the threshold into the cold and dark.

"Oh, er, sorry," replied Nisha, appearing uncomfortable. "I have something I need to do."

"Sure," said Chrissie. "Of course, sorry."

"No," said Nisha, reaching out to touch Chrissie's cheek, "don't be sorry. Honestly, there's really nothing I'd rather do. I just need to go and sort something this evening."

"Sure," repeated Chrissie, her voice flat. Her heart felt flat, too. Like Nisha was slipping away. "I might have a quick one before I go home," she said, deciding that whether or not she had an after-work drink wasn't down to Nisha.

"You do that," said Nisha, leaning over to kiss her cheek. "See you bright and early tomorrow."

"Yeah," said Chrissie, trying hard to smile, and failing.

Ten minutes later she sat down in the bar, feeling like she stuck out a little on her own. She pulled out her phone and messaged Rae to ask if they wanted a cheeky snifter. Her friend was online and replied swiftly. "Sorry, Chrissie, I've got something on this eve. Maybe at the weekend?"

Chrissie sighed. No doubt Rae was with Clodagh. Lucky them. It would just be her this evening. Well, she wasn't going to let that stop her. She needed to trust herself, to plough her own furrow – another expression of her dad's. She ordered herself a glass of Rioja and sat down in the quiet upstairs section. She thought about Don and what he might have said to her, if he'd been here.

Chrissie smiled to herself. To start with, her Brummie father would have ordered himself a pint of bitter and complained about her drinking something as refined as wine.

One thing she knew, though, was he'd have given her the same advice as he had all those years ago: that she needed to do the right thing for her. He would have told her that if it was meant to work out, it would. She needed to have faith that somehow, she would find her way through.

"You look very deep in thought, bab," came the rasping voice of the parish vicar.

"Oh, hi, Rebecca, sorry. I was miles away," said Chrissie.

"No need to be sorry, bab, you do you. Fancy company?" Rebecca was wearing a big black puffer jacket, and looked a little like a gangster. "Do say 'no' if you'd rather be alone."

"Company would be lovely," said Chrissie. "Really, please do join me."

"Excellent. I'll be back shortly," said Rebecca, returning a few minutes later with a double vodka tonic.

"How did you know you wanted to be a vicar?" asked Chrissie.

"Goodness, this is like being interviewed by the diocese all over again," Rebecca chuckled.

"Sorry, I…" started Chrissie, but Rebecca waved her hand.

"Honestly, I suppose no one knows what they want to do for sure, or what the right path is. To me, it just felt right. I knew I needed to follow my faith, and I knew I needed to serve other people. Becoming a vicar was the best way to do that," said the older woman, before taking a slug of her drink. "I needed that. One of the volunteers engaged me in a long conversation about flower arranging earlier, and after a long day, I could have done without that." She looked up. "May God forgive me, although I suspect even He would have grown bored after twenty minutes of it."

Chrissie laughed. "I guess whatever you choose, there's always something that gets on your nerves."

"Indeed. So, tell me about what's been going on at the school, then. You've been super busy these last few weeks, and I've heard whispers of an inspection."

"Oh heavens, yes. Do they do that in churches?" asked Chrissie.

"Sort of, although I tend to work on the basis that really the only person who can inspect me is God, and He doesn't tend to send reports to anyone about what He thinks, thank goodness," said Rebecca.

They both laughed, and Chrissie updated her friend on the latest developments.

Chapter Fifty-Six

"Right-oh everyone," said Mrs Hemingway, with all the confidence of a Naval Commander. "We all know what we need to do. Just go out there and do your best."

The staff team set their faces into grim smiles and left the staff room. The inspectors had already arrived, and had set up base in an empty classroom on the other side of the school. They now had the right to pop up in any class at any time, and inspect the quality of the teaching and talk to the children.

Nisha and Chrissie made their way to their classroom, which had been cleaned to within an inch of its life, courtesy of the school's loyal cleaners who had become part of the team ready to respond to the inspection.

"We just need to do our thing," said Nisha. "Mrs H is right."

"Yep," agreed Chrissie, walking over to the external classroom door where pupils were clamouring to be let in. "Now then, children," she said as she opened the door. "Today, we are going to be our absolute best selves."

"Why, miss?" asked Hardev.

"Cos of the stinky inspectors," replied Dottie, at the top of her voice. It was as if she knew that at that moment a grey-haired man in an ill-fitting suit was entering the class-room via the other door.

"Good morning," said Nisha, rushing towards the inspector and leaving Chrissie to finish the whispered pep talk for the class.

Once the register had been taken, it was literacy hour, and the children cracked on with work that they might or might not have already done a few days earlier, in a bid to ensure none of them felt overwhelmed by something new.

Chrissie and Nisha roamed the room, checking in with the pupils, who were working in an unnatural silence. It was helpful for first impressions, but slightly unnerving to Chrissie who had never known this group so quiet.

They met strategically at the furthest point of the room from the inspector, and Nisha grabbed a book from the shelf as if to show it to Chrissie. "Well, at least we're getting our bit out of the way early doors," she whispered.

Chrissie pointed at a picture of a frog in the book as she whispered back, "Yes, although the silence in this room is making me nervous."

Nisha smothered a giggle and put the book back on the shelf before heading over to help Francis, whose hand had gone up.

Chrissie hovered by Hardev, who, based on past experience, was the pupil most likely to do something ridiculous. But for once, he had his head down and was concentrating on his work.

The staffroom was quiet at lunchtime, as so many

teachers had opted to continue with prep in their class-rooms. Chrissie was on playground duty, so she had donned her thick coat and was walking around clutching her thermal cup of tea and keeping the children in order. Meanwhile Nisha was triple-checking the paperwork that the inspectors would spend the evening examining.

"Last one to the pub's a green turd," said Dan as the end-of-the-day huddle broke up.

"Very funny," said Chrissie, but she and Nisha both followed him.

It was midweek, so the Vine was quiet. It was a good antidote to the last few days. "I'm not having much to drink," said Nisha. "We have another day of this tomorrow."

"Yeah, I know," agreed Dan. "Just a cheeky half to ease the nerves and help us relax."

"Yep, sounds ideal," said Chrissie. Her eyes met Nisha's, who smiled at her. Nisha seemed more present today, less distracted. She'd obviously made up her mind. Chrissie knew this might be the beginning of the end for them, and she tried to push the thought away.

Chapter Fifty-Seven

At three o'clock on Friday afternoon, the children left school, and the staff got away from the site quicker than they ever had before. The inspectors had departed earlier that day, having left Mrs Hemingway with a verbal update. She had explained she wasn't able to share what she'd been told, as it was still to be confirmed, but had added with a wink that she was sure all the teaching staff would have an 'outstanding' weekend. This had resulted in a cheer in the staff room.

"I guess we should have that talk," said Chrissie, as she and Nisha left school for the last time that week.

"We should," said Nisha. Her face was serious but unreadable. Chrissie had had plenty of time to think, and she already knew what she wanted to say, in spite of the fatigue of the hardest working week of her life. "Is it ok if we go back to yours?"

"Yes, of course," said Chrissie.

"My place is still covered in paperwork from the inspection prep, and I don't think I can face it right now."

Chrissie took Nisha's hand and wondered if they'd be doing this walk together again after the Christmas break.

Chrissie's house was cold, so the first thing she did was put the heating on. "I know it's only mid-afternoon," she said, "but in the circumstances, I think it would be reasonable for us to have one glass of wine."

"Or perhaps more," suggested Nisha with a grin.

They settled themselves under a blanket on the sofa with their wine. Chrissie put her arm around Nisha and spoke first. "Ok, Nisha. I know you have things to say. But I need to say things, too."

"You do?" said Nisha.

"Yes. I've done a lot of thinking, and I want to be honest with you."

Nisha swallowed. "Ok. I'm not going to lie, you're making me a bit nervous."

"Sorry. Look, I'll just say it. I'm not going to come to London with you. The offer of a training place is one I simply can't turn down." Chrissie turned her head to look at Nisha as she spoke. "But I love you, and I want to be with you. Both of those things are true. And while I have abandoned my 'rules'," she continued, using air quotes, "I do need to hold onto myself. It took me a long time to build my life in Birmingham back up after I burned it to the ground. I need to stay here and continue to put down my roots."

Nisha opened her mouth to speak, her brows furrowed. "Sorry, please," said Chrissie. "Can you just let me finish? This isn't easy."

Nisha pursed her lips and nodded.

"It's only fair I tell you that I have accepted that training place here, and I will be staying here. Now what that means for us, is something we can work through. I'm not sure how a distance relationship would work, because I know you'll be crazy busy in your first headship, and I'll be up to my eyes in college work. I do think we owe it to ourselves to try, though," said Chrissie. In her heart, she knew it would place huge pressure on their fledgling romance. But she also knew she couldn't give that romance up.

"Well," said Nisha, "that's a lot." She took a sip from her drink. "I have to tell you, I really don't want to do a distance relationship."

Chrissie's heart plummeted as Nisha continued.

"I was involved in one years ago. I was with this woman for about two years. We lived a hundred miles apart. We thought we could make it work, but it really was just such hard work. I think even if you love each other, it puts too much pressure on a relationship. I don't want to do that to you."

Chrissie nodded and looked down into her lap, not wanting to show the tears that were beginning to pool in her eyes. She appreciated Nisha's honesty, but it was painful. So they were to be ships that passed in the night, after all. Friends for a season.

"So I have come to a decision," said Nisha, her own eyes brimming with tears. She put a hand on Chrissie's bowed shoulder. Chrissie tried and failed to cover a sob, trying not to imagine what life would be like after Christmas, with no Nisha.

"I'm not going," said Nisha quietly.

"What?" said Chrissie in shock, bringing her head up and almost head-butting Nisha.

"Steady!" said Nisha. "I've turned down the job."

"But you said it yourself. This is the opportunity of a lifetime, and it's your chance to put things right after you ran away from London," said Chrissie, trying to make sense of what she was hearing.

"Well, it seems I have a high class problem. I've been given two opportunities of a lifetime. The first one is that job. But the more important one is you. I let you go once, I ran away from you once, and I realised this week that if I went to London I'd be running away again. Running away from taking this opportunity, just in case we didn't work out. I realised that sometimes you leave a situation because you're ready to go. It's not always running away. And the last thing I wanted to do was run out on you again. We have a chance to be happy, and I owe it to us both to take that chance," Nisha concluded, following up her words with a generous mouthful of wine.

"Wow," said Chrissie. "You've done a load of thinking."

"Yes," agreed Nisha. She gave Chrissie a sheepish smile. "I must confess, I had a little bit of help."

"You did?" said Chrissie.

"Yes. Rae. You remember the other night when you wanted to go for a drink? Well, I met up with Rae. We really hit it off that night in the Vine, with Clodagh, and I remembered how much you say they've helped you sort out your thoughts. For someone so young, they always sounded so wise. I don't have loads of friends here yet, and so I dropped them a line. They were amazing."

Chrissie grinned. "They really are. I feel so lucky to have them as my friend. Even more so now, if they've helped you come to this decision. But are you sure this is really the right thing for you?"

Nisha stared at her as she continued.

"I would hate to hold you back," Chrissie said. "What if this didn't work out? I'd hate for you to resent me."

"I could never resent you, Chris," Nisha told her, her eyes wet. "Rae reminded me that if there are opportunities in London, there will be opportunities in Birmingham.

Maybe even in our own school at some point – although I fully accept Mrs H will never retire."

Chrissie laughed. "Not a chance. Did you talk to Mrs H about it?"

"Yes," said Nisha. "I did. She actually gave me some good advice herself, and told me I needed to make the right decision for me. So I called Jake last night and told him that I really appreciated the job offer, but that I was turning it down."

"You're kidding?" said Chrissie, shocked that so much had happened without her even knowing.

"I'm not. I love you," said Nisha, "and this time I'm going to stick around and see what happens next."

"I love you too," said Chrissie, taking both their wine glasses and placing them on a side table, before leaning forward and kissing Nisha. As she did so, she remembered all the times they had kissed before, from that first time in the tent, to the time in the rain, and all the times in Paris.

This wasn't the beginning of the end. It was the start of the beginning.

Chapter Fifty-Eight

SEVEN MOTHS LATER

The sun was streaming through the windows of the staff room. Chrissie was drinking tea and eating her packed lunch beside Nisha and Dan, as was their daily routine, unless one of them had playground duty.

"So," said Dan, "it's your last day as a TA. How does that feel?"

"Weird," Chrissie replied. "Really weird."

"I can imagine," said Nisha, who wore an excitable smile.

"What's up with you?" asked Chrissie.

"Oh, nothing," said Nisha, pretending to absorb herself in her sandwich.

"Nonsense," said Chrissie, "I'll make you tell me later."

"Ladies, please," said Dan. "I don't want to hear anything about your bedtime adventures."

Chrissie and Nisha laughed. "Prude," said Nisha.

"That's me," said Dan, "all sweet and innocent."

"Hmm," said Chrissie. "I doubt that."

"Good afternoon, everyone," said Mrs Hemingway,

strolling into the staffroom. "It's been a really successful academic year, entirely thanks to all of you. Thank you."

A round of applause went round the room, and Nisha and Chrissie locked eyes, knowing that they would remember this year for much more than what had happened at work.

"And before I send you off for the summer break, I have an announcement to make." The teachers quietened down to hear what their boss had to say. "As you all know, Mr Smart has taken early retirement this term. We will miss him, and everything he has brought to the school, but this leaves us with a vacancy in the Senior Leadership Team. I am therefore delighted to announce that our new deputy head teacher as of next term will be Ms Rajan."

The room erupted into applause, which was fortunate as Chrissie squealed, "Oh my God," at Nisha at the top of her voice. "Why didn't you tell me?"

"I was a bit superstitious," said Nisha, "and I wasn't sure I would get it. There were a couple of really good candidates up for the job. I only found out myself this morning."

"That is incredible. Well done!" said Chrissie.

"But just so you know, I won't be going easy on you next year, as I'll be your boss now," Nisha told her, waggling her eyebrows.

"Oh God," said Dan, "yet more double entendres. Put your whip away, Ms Rajan, please."

"In your dreams," said Nisha, before turning back to Chrissie, who threw her arms around her.

"I knew this would work out," said Chrissie.

"Me too," Nisha agreed.

"So," asked Dan, "do you two have plans for the summer?"

Nisha and Chrissie grinned at him and spoke at the same time. "Paris."

He laughed. "Presumably without any children."

"Exactly," they said.

———

I hope you enjoyed *Don't Fall in Love (and how to break the rules)*.

Do you want to find out what happens next for Chrissie and Nisha? You can download a free epilogue from my website.

If you'd like to receive my newsletter, you can sign up at: www.sallybrooksauthor.com

Sally Brooks

Faking It (and falling in love)

When Philippa comes out at 46, she has no idea what to expect. Juggling a high-powered job as a family lawyer, lone-parenting a 10-year-old daughter and navigating her new life push her to the limit. She doesn't have time to fall in love, but when she meets carefree graphic designer Alex at a professional networking event, people think they are a couple. For both women this is a convenient way to present themselves to the world, so they keep up the pretense.

To Philippa's surprise, her feelings for Alex start to grow, but the graphic designer doesn't want to settle down with anyone... so their fake relationship status can't become real.

But when Alex comes to Philippa with a problem that only she can help with, things get complicated. Can Philippa resist her growing feelings towards Alex while trying to help her gain access to her child? Or should Philippa steer clear of Alex and her hedonistic lifestyle for the benefit of her own daughter?

Don't miss this romantic comedy with heart-felt

moments about navigating coming out later in life, the perils of lone-parenting and falling in love when you least expect it, from the author of *Swiping Right (and other disasters)* and *Don't Fall in Love (and how to break the rules)*.

Order *Faking It (and falling in love)* now!

Also by Sally Brooks

The Second Chance Chronicles

Swiping Right (and other disasters)

Don't Fall in Love (and how to break the rules)

Faking It (and falling in love)

The Shadow Series

Her Shadow: A Story of Love, Loss and Politics

Theatre of Shadows: Power, Politics and Passion

Four Movements: Fifty Years, Four People, One Piano

Buy now from book retailers.

Printed in Great Britain
by Amazon